The Watchers
Fall From Grace

by
Amanda Zarovsky

Happy Duck Publishing
PO Box 607
Belle, MO 65013

Genre: Fantasy Fiction
ISBN: 978-0-9861182-8-9
Second Edition.

This book is for my children and husband. Thank you for being my unshakable foundation and letting me build my dream.

ACKNOWLEDGEMENTS

I want to thank my husband James for his love and support, always believing in me, and encouraging me to follow my dreams. Most of all I want to thank him for being there in thick and thin, bad and good, and highs and lows.

I want to thank my sister Melody for always believing in me and pushing me to follow my dream. For all the nights that she would sit at the foot of my bed as teenagers, anxiously waiting for the next page of my story.

I want to thank my brother Scotty who always treated me more like his best friend instead of his sister. Who always knew that I would become someone, even when I doubted myself.

I want to thank my children Jadyn, Joey, Eli, Gracey, Taylor, and Brooklin for showing me what patience and perseverance is and also for believing in me.

I want to thank my parents for never giving up on me and putting up with a very defiant child from day one. You always knew that defiance would come in handy later in life... and it did!

To Lucinda, who introduced me to Edward. I owe you so much!

To my friends who are like family to me: Sonia, Jana, Beth, Amanda (my relief fighter, RIP), Liz, Emily, and so many more. Without your support and love, I don't think I would have made it this far.

To my nieces and nephews for all the laughter, and a few tears, and reminding me what being young is all about.

To everyone who has supported me and stood behind me, thank you. I might have given up by now if it weren't for you.

To a handful of singers and musicians that inspired me along the way: Bigbang, BTS, Shinee, EXO, VIXX, CL, Jesse, Got7, Seventeen, Monstax, and many more in the Kpop industry. A very special thanks to Kwon Jiyong (AKA G Dragon) for being my number one inspiration and for teaching me that with enough hard work and persistence I could achieve anything.

I want to dedicate this book to Kim Jong Hyun. Thank you

for all the beautiful music you gave us. May you rest in eternal peace.

To my fans, thank you. I started out with a dream. Now this is one thing I can finally, after 30 years, scratch off my bucket list. I love you all!

PROLOGUE

The pitch blackness of the sky was chased away by streaks of lightning from the approaching storm. The bleating of creatures, great and small, added to the cacophony that was enveloping the world. Shepherds clung to their families while thunder exploded from above, sending their flocks stampeding through the mountains and valleys.

Violent winds screeched from the corners of every nation, using the smallest of debris to flay exposed skin open with devastating effect. Caravans ground to a halt. Houses shook and all men trembled and prayed for release from the rage nature had unleashed upon them.

As heads were covered to avoid storms, as knees were bent to withstand the strength of the wind, as humanity cried out for salvation for whatever they had done to anger the gods, no eyes were looking skyward. If ones senses had been able to withstand the forces causing such disaster they would have witnessed the purging of Heaven. They would have seen streaks of colored fire being hurled toward Earth with such force that only the creators could be responsible. Each fiery streak was a being cast out of paradise.

As the fallen descended to Earth, banished from their heavenly home, their anger and rage grew more intense than the storm that threatened mankind. Many of the fallen were angry and resentful towards humans, a recent creation that had taken their place of honor as the most beloved creatures in the eyes of the creators.

Slowly, the storms anger was spent. Man emerged from his

dwellings to rebuild and found himself no longer alone. Celestial beings, now stripped of most of their power, walked among them. They held many names, but favored the mantle of watchers. That was what their heavenly creators had called them. Watchers; pulled into existence and loved by their celestial architects.

Azazel, a mighty and powerful angel at the forefront of the rebellion in Heaven; Ruax, a magnificent angel with a great lust for human blood, and many more would arrive on earth to live among their hated enemies. Yet some of them realized their sins and sought to protect mankind from their evil brethren.

It was Azazel who first suggested that the angels take human women as wives. In doing this he committed an unforgiving sin against the gods. From this unholy union an evil race was born, the nephilim. They went on to bear their own children with angels, who were even darker and more sinister than their parents. Eventually their numbers were so great they could not be counted. These offspring would come to be known as vampires.

Azazel began to teach mankind how to build weapons and wage war with one another. He stirred the flames of hate in hopes that humans would destroy themselves. For this he was banished by the creators to deep inside of a mountain to await judgment during the end of times.

The vampires, rebellious in nature, defied all orders of their parents and the gods. The most sacred commandment being ritualistic blood sacrifices. Instead of offering the blood up to the gods as humans had done before to appease them, the vampires took of the blood themselves.

In retribution the angered gods cursed the land with diseases of the blood; so that any who would partake in the blood would fall ill and eventually die.

Many of the vampires were destroyed by this means. Others became stronger. But, in time, there were also some who rebelled against their own kind. These set out to rid the earth of the watchers and free mankind from the clutches of their evil.

CHAPTER ONE
The Mission

Sunset this time of the year was always beautiful. A pale gray sky curtained a part of the earth as equally pale and almost as lifeless as the crypts to which the dead lay. I knew the days would be short now; darkness would consume the light much earlier than in previous months. It was during this time that creatures of the night would come out from the depths to do one of three things; feed, breed, or rebel.

I was a part of that last group. Though we did feed, as all living and semi-living beings must, breeding was optional. Most of us were repulsed by every creature we came across that we remained celibate, myself included except for the rare exception.

There were dangers out there, especially for us creatures of the night. Things imposed by the gods that we feared. We were not the ones who brought this upon the Earth, but we were equally punished for what our fathers had done.

Legends had always portrayed my kind as inherently evil. The truth is we were byproducts of an evil source. As children of the nephilim, we were born with aspects of the power of our fathers and grandfathers. Many of my kind knew several secrets of the universe; the astrological signs given to us by the gods to guide and direct us and the magic which every creature on earth possessed, though few knew how to use.

While the watchers had been cursed to this land for their rebellion, and their children the nephilim branded the vilest and most evil race to be born from the daughters of men, the next generation of demons had in fact turned away from most of the evil imprinted on us by our grandfathers.

Most of us were sick of seeing our names run through the

mud for something we didn't even do and, on this day, many of us gathered to discuss our plans to take down the watchers and restore humanity to what it once was. Before the watchers were forced here and defiled humans; a world with harmony and balance.

Most of the nephilim were brutes that would kill anyone or anything just for the taste of blood.

Some vampires weren't exactly cuddly bunnies that you'd invite over to your dear sweet grandma's house, either. There were those who were absolute tyrants and would feed off the necks of whomever they wanted to, but most of us were rather peaceful and non-aggressive.

Throughout history, nephilim bred with humans, they bore children, and then their children bred with humans until eventually our blood line of immortality nearly ended. There were a select few who were sired from existing nephilim and angels, but without the third generation vampires breeding and bearing children we were the last of our kind. We, the Order of Spera, intended to keep it that way.

The Order had recently declared that no new vampires would be sired and no vampire was permitted to breed with a human or angel ever again in order to keep our race as pure as we could and to prevent our immortality from being bred out. This was hard for some, but it was not entirely difficult for me. I viewed mortals as weak and filthy beings with no knowledge of anything beyond their struggle to survive. They were like peasants to me. I had very little physical desires for them at all.

I always found it rather funny that mortals had spent centuries trying to unlock the secrets of immortality, of magic, and the universe. But yet my kind was born with it. My angelic ancestors had watched the fall of humanity in the Garden of Eden, as man and woman had both become prey to the lures of the watchers. They were so beautiful and magnificent that no mortal willpower could stand against them. It's like seeing that one person that gets in your head and you can imagine yourself intimate with them day after day, never getting enough; and with each drink from their wicked goblet, the hunger and thirst would only increase. For this reason the humans had never been able to resist them. They become so enthralled to such majestic creatures that they did not even realize they were slaves.

Instead of helping men achieve the knowledge and the power of the gods, the watchers began to exploit humans for their own purpose. They caused the nephilim to fight among them and to create wars all over the earth. They would use their human slaves to fight their battles for them, but the wars never seemed to end.

The watchers did not want humans to learn the secrets of the universe, their own powers, and so on. They feared it would warp their minds and judgment and make them more resistant to the watchers' power and authority. So they devised a plan to shape the way humans believed. They successfully created various religions that would appease the humans. What they did not know was that the watchers were clever and incorporated a lot of truth in these fables such as a monotheism theory and boundaries on love and relationships, even down to fighting over land. That was all created by the watchers to divide the people up since mankind had committed the ultimate act of betrayal against the gods and bred with the fallen angels. We were their punishment.

It came back to bite us when they started killing us. Thousands of us slaughtered in the name of religions that my ancestors helped create, but there was no stopping it now. The only way to put an end to it would be to destroy the watchers and the nephilim; restore the humans to what they were before the watchers were cast down from the heavens. Most would forget over time, their magic and their will. But a few never would. Those mortals were very important to us because they were the key to ending this war.

I really didn't care. The mortals could all fight until only a few of them remained and it would be fine by me. While I did not raise my hand to any of them, curse them, or cause harm of any sort, I felt the planet would be better if most of them weren't here. But the Order refused to allow that thought into any of our heads. The mortals had to be protected, like sheep in a field.

On this night, just as the sun settled behind the cityscape, I ascended from my slumber deep within the earth. I made my way to the surface where the routine flow of human traffic awaited me. I hated the city for all of its noise and lights. But even in the most well-lit part of the city, I could remain completely hidden. Thank the gods for New York, no one seemed to notice weirdos. In the country, I would likely get shot.

As I made my way down the sidewalk towards our meeting place, I looked at the faces of each person that passed me by. Most were empty, emotionless; as if they bore no soul at all. They were so beat down and brainwashed that they could not see that the chains that bound them were their own beliefs and lack of will. All they had to do was open their eyes to the truths instilled in their souls, but they wouldn't. They had been convinced that this is how humans must survive, by being the slaves of another. It was in that moment I inhaled a deep breath, and whispered a thank you to my mother that chose to have me by a angel. I really do not think I would be able to live like a human; enslaved to inanimate objects, by false ideas and religions, and by being powerless.

My gaze was drawn to something, a shadow up against a building. It was an old, frail man sitting with his back to the wall with a look of sorrow and of complete failure on his face. He said nothing as he looked up at me when I slowed my pace in front of him.

Our appearances were polar opposite. He may have once been a tall man, but age had bent and warped his frame. I was just under six feet tall and towered over him. My skin was a flawless, caramel tone; his clung to his bones, cracked by weather and years of hard living.

Gray hair hung past his forehead and rested lightly against lean cheeks. A disheveled beard clung to his face, soaked with the remains of whatever food he had managed to scavenge. I was clean shaven, with my black layered hair barely gracing my shoulders.

His clothes were stained beyond any identification of color. His shoes held together by nothing more than black electrical tape. On this night I had donned black faux leather pants, a tight baby blue shirt, and a pair of studded boots that made me seem tougher than I wanted anyone to know that I was. I had a perfect blend of douche bag and loser rock star going for me.

He gazed up at me, his pupils wide and frightened. He appeared not to have known happiness in a very long time. Our eyes were so different from each other as well. Mine were a smooth, distinct almond-shaped while his sagged with age so badly one could hardly tell his ancestry.

I could not look away from him. My compassion began to eat at me and I reached into my pocket for some coins and dollars that I kept just in case my mortal appearance had use of them. The time was now. I bent down and placed all the money that I had in his open palm. I felt a disturbing surge of energy corse through my body I could see the tears in his eyes, the years of hurt and torment that only the gods could possibly know about. For a moment our eyes were deadlocked. He seemed to speak to me without words and what he seemed to say was 'Save us'. I felt very depressed all of a sudden and realized I needed to get away from him as soon as I could. I stood to my feet, and nodded to the man, and began once more on my way to the meeting place. As soon as I had put some distance between us, the uneasy feeling that had suddenly consumed me was now slowly fading.

Something about that old man got to me. No mortal had ever done that before. The moment that he touched my hand, I could feel every ounce of his pain. It was overwhelming, even for me, but this man somehow dealt with it. He was strong despite his weak appearance.

So much pain and despair around me, and so needless. They already possessed everything that they needed in this life, but they refused to acknowledge it. I really believe some of them were scared of the truth and did everything possible to destroy it. It made me really sad.

I finally reached my destination, a marbled cottage that was completely invisible to the average person. They did not see it because they did not want to see. They did not see because of their delusions and by the simple act of not believing. They didn't want to believe that we existed, therefore in their minds, we did not. We were just scary stories parents told their children to trick them into behaving. In other words, we were used to make slaves out of children.

I carefully made my way up the many steps leading to the doorway. I could hear the low rumble of chatter as I approached. They had started the meeting without me. At the door I was greeted by scorned looks and hisses of disapproval. I knew those looks. I had seen them every time I had been late, which was mostly always.

The prefect, a handsome vampire with bright amber eyes, glared at me as I entered. "Lafayette, I see you finally decided to join us."

I wanted to reply something sarcastic, but this was neither the time nor place to do such a thing, nor was the prefect the type of person to appreciate my cynicism. "Sorry I'm late. I had a bit of a hang up."

"Find something useless to waste our time on?" It was Belfore who spoke, one vampire I would love to drain the last drop of blood from then carve him up like a side of beef and serve him up like a Kosher Saturday dinner. I hated that guy. He was rude, sarcastic, cruel, and just a pain in the ass. He was the type of vampire that thought he was above everyone. He seemed to possess a god complex as well and thought that he could charm everyone he came near. The only reaction he envoked in me was a gag reflex.

I discreetly posed my middle finger in his direction and he cracked a smirk at me. *Yeah, laugh it up asshole. One day… just one day.*

"Enough!" the prefect exploded in a stern voice, obviously seeing the squabble going on silently between me and Belfore. "We have enough problems without you two wanting to kill each other." He stared at me in a way that made me feel remorseful of my own childish actions.

"An informant brings dire news: the watchers are aware of our plans. Do you understand what this means?"

Informant? My mind became filled with questions as to who the prefect was using to gather such intel.

The prefect leaned forward and, as if he had read my mind at that moment, says in a slightly hushed toned, "It means that there is a traitor among the order."

The room filled with chatter as fellow vampires expressed their concern of who that might be. Those accused quickly responded with objections to steer the suspicion away from them. I just sat quietly and observed each person and their body language. I noted a few that seemed unusually nervous. I kept that to myself. If there was a snitch in our midst, I would rather observe them than draw out anyone in particular.

The prefect continued once the initial outcry silenced, "Rumor has it that many of them are in Europe at the moment; wearing the guise of the ruling class. Apparently they are organizing a large scale meeting in England. The rulers of this world are plotting to seize control of the world's most valuable resources. They are expanding the reach of their powers even into the pit that they may control the flow of souls. Transport has been prepared. You will all be divided up into teams of three. Your assignments are to gather intelligence on enemy strategies. Keep a low profile. Discover their plans and, if necessary, deal with it."

Again this stirred the room to a nervous chatter regarding the commands of the prefect. *Deal with it? Was this an order to kill?*

"And how do you propose we do this?" Belfore spoke up with his usual sarcastic tone.

The prefect cleared his throat and glanced around at everyone. "I can't tell you how. Each action will depend on the situation. So assess the situation and come to a conclusion based on what you feel is the best course of action. But remember, a lot of these watchers are well respected members of every government position and high court that you can think of. The humans support them. They really believe these watchers have their best interests at heart."

Although his intentions seemed legitimate and well thought out, this would be no easy task. He was putting a lot of us at great risk with this task. Nonetheless, it had to be done. We were the only ones that could do it. I was apprehensive about this notion and, quite honestly, I had no idea where to even start. But the prefect was way ahead of me on that one.

"Lafayette, you, Belfore, and Thia will head to the UK. There are many watchers there. I cannot tell you specifically where they are, just that they are hidden among the rich and powerful."

Thia looked up from where she sat across from me and mimicked the same objectional look on my face. I smiled slightly to her to which she rebuffed with a heavy sigh and eye roll. She did look amazing though. I felt her attire was a bit on the risqué side but nonetheless beautiful. She was too beautiful, actually; as if she just didn't fit in with a group of vampires. Her appearance was very angelic-like in nature. As I briefly caught myself thinking of her as just a beautiful woman, I scolded myself. We weren't friends. We hardly got along at all, though I had no logical reason why.

I didn't know her all that well, though we had worked together a few times before. She was a quiet, attractive sort and never seemed to question the authority of the prefect. She almost seemed too willing and acquiescent of all he said and that troubled me. Personally, I didn't take orders kindly. I would do something if asked, but I did not do well with commands. I was an arrogant bastard most of the time.

"There is one other thing."

Everyone grew silent to hear what else he had to say. "There is an item that was stolen from us a long time ago. It may seem insignificant, but it is very valuable to our existence. It is a rare gem, a quartz stone, if you will."

And now he had us on a treasure hunt, great!

"And what does this gem look like?" Belfore leaned forward in his chair.

"You will know when you find it. It possesses great power in the hands of the one who wields it. In the right hands, it can save mankind. In the wrong hands, it will destroy them. I need you to find it at all costs, and bring it back to me."

Well, this should be easy. All we have to do is search the entire world for some quartz rock. Yeah, shouldn't be hard at all.

My thoughts drifted to other things as the prefect grouped more teams together and gave them their orders. I was pleased that he was sending my team to the UK. I had secretly hoped he wouldn't send us to some desert. It wasn't exactly my kind of place. I had really dry skin and needed a damp climate.

The jokes you hear about the Royal Family bloodline being that of vampires, well, it isn't entirely fictional. Though there were a few decent and moral members of the Royals, most of them were life sucking leeches full of greed, wealth, and power. I was certain a few watchers were hiding among them.

Part of our success would lie in man. If they were to ever awaken from their dumbed-down comatose state of mind, realize their inner powers and strengths, the watchers would have no more control over them. Part of this system of control was weaking the mind and the will of the humans. I didn't have much faith in humans though. Over the centuries, they have only proven to become weaker; submitting to even the slightest command of authority. Humans had lost the will to govern or dictate their own lives and entrusted it with those they perceived as their superiors. Our survival depended on the humans reclaiming their own inner powers which would in turn weaken those trying to manipulate and control them.

The watchers had strategically placed one of their own in every nation on earth. They were creating sort of a chessboard and at the right moment; checkmate. They had power beyond all reason and understanding and very few who attempted to take them down had survived.

The masters that they served were quickly destroying the earth that we all inhabited. All of the natural resources were being drained from this system of hierarchy. People were starving all over the world. They were strewn about like rubbish on the streets. And they were quickly losing the will to live and fight against it anymore. Those in absolute power wished to control every single person on earth and to strip them of everything vital to survival so that they would go crawling to them and begging for mercy, as if the powers that be were gods.

The watchers hid in the shadows of the night, planning their takeovers within their circle of trusted members; which included many humans who were completely unaware of the watchers true identities or purpose. They relied heavily on the obscurity of human knowledge. We had to act quickly to reinstate man's power and knowledge that was given to the first human on earth; who so willingly had traded it for the pleasure promised by the watchers; and in doing so, traded his very soul to the same beings that modern day religious leaders warned them about. Since that day, man has entertained the idea of redemption, to cleanse them from the dreadful future they were all doomed to. They taught their children to fear the god of their faith, and that all were condemned for what their ancestors had done. This desire to be redeemed only created panic among men; it made them confrontational and sometimes violent, to anyone who challenged their obscure beliefs.

But this was the plan from the start; initiated by the watchers, to drive mankind into submission out of fear that their souls would be condemned if they did not. It was working. Man had never been more unstable and insecure with themselves in all of the history of the world. They were dividing themselves up and becoming easy targets of the powers that be to take full control.

With each member of the order instructed on where to go, the meeting was adjourned. Everyone began to depart on their own quests and I did not hesitate to leave the room in hopes Belfore and Thia would not follow. Belfore, being the self-indulged ass that I knew him to be, was in no hurry to catch up with me and play follow-the-leader. I suppose he intended to defy the orders of the prefect and venture out on his own.

This was fine by me. His presence only magnified any emotion in any situation and I felt that it was better for my own success if he simply did not tag along. Thia, on the other hand, would never defy the commands of the Order and thus, followed me to the door.

"Lafayette, just a minute," I heard the prefect say as the others quickly left the room. I turned to face him as Thia paused for a second before proceeding out of the door.

"I need you to do something for me," the prefect continued. I hummed an aknolwedgement and nodded. "While your mission is still pretty much the same as the others, it's your team I want to really find the pendent."

"Why me?"

The prefect smiled. "You're not like the others, Lafayette. You are, shall we say, a bit more rebellious in nature. You're not the type to go with the flow, take orders, or submit to authority. You're also not as susceptible to most forms of supernatural powers. Which is why you may not be as greatly effected by the powers of the pendent."

"And what *is* this pendent? What's it's purpose?"

He sighed and turned away from me. "That's not important. What is important is that it never gets into the wrong hands and is brought back to me as quickly as possible."

"You're essentially asking me to find a needle in a haystack, you know that? You want me to scour the entire planet in search of a rock."

"No. I am sending you to England where I know it's being guarded by its host. When you find it, you will know. The energy from it alone will be felt from miles away."

I huffed a deep sigh and he turned facing me. "Don't fail me, Lafayette. If this pendent gets into the wrong hands we are all doomed."

This increased my anxiety and apprehension of the mission now. I could not afford to fail, yet I wasn't so confident of myself.

I walked along the sidewalk with Thia trailing behind me. I pretended to not acknowledge her and hoped she would get the picture and move on. Alas, I was wrong.

I stopped abruptly. "Thia. You wish to join me?"

"It is the command of the prefect that I accompany you." Her soft voice was stern and adamant.

I turned to face her and was immediately again captured by her astounding beauty. She was small and sort of frail in appearance. Nonetheless, she was a fearless fighter who was not to be reckoned with.

"There are great dangers where I'm going." I tried to discourage her from following me. But I knew that she was as stubborn as I was and my efforts would be futile.

"Which is why you need me!" she snapped in a firm and abrasive tone.

I had to hand it to her, she was very confident; perhaps maybe even a little cocky, but I knew that she was strong and could take on any task that the order instructed her on. The flight to England would be a rather long and painfully dull one. To have a bit of company with her charm and intellect would be refreshing. I choked up the courage to admit that she was right, and that I did indeed need her on this quest.

Though we were immortal beings with great power, an ability none of us had acquired was flying. The few who had attempted it had become nice little crimson ink blots on the pavement. This certainly had almost blown our covers a few times by those who had witnessed such a terrible display of recklessness. It was quite difficult to explain to the medical examiners how we would suddenly spring to life and leap off the table as if we had only fallen and bumped our bottoms.

Normally those who attempted such daring acts had simply convinced the medical personnel that they were only dazed and confused and the medical examiners were just too stunned to accept what they had witnessed and typically preferred to remain hush about it.

Speaking such things would almost certainly land them in a mental facility somewhere on an island far from civilized life. It is also important to note that the idiots who had tempted fate with their less than perfect flight capabilities were often reprimanded by the order. Oftentimes they would be reassigned to desk duty.

"I see that I will not be able to convince you to join one of the other teams, eh?" I made my last attempt to sway her, which I knew that I would not be successful at.

"No you will not. It is by directive of the order that I assist you on this mission. And I cannot defy those orders."

Very determined... very... female-like...

I sighed in defeat and stepped closer to her. "Then you must listen to me at all times. You must do as I say, understand?"

"Yes, except for the 'do as I say' bit. I serve no one but the order. My instructions are from them alone."

I drew her close to me and lowered my tone. "There are forces at work here that you have never known. I am not saying to serve me. I am saying to trust me not to steer you wrong. I have a lot of experience with these forces and I consider myself more equipped than you to handle them."

She gazed into my eyes and a firm grin stretched her facial features to abnormal proportions. "You keep telling yourself that, Lafayette. I will listen to you. I will act on what I feel is appropriate according to the order's wishes, but you will not boss me around like your own personal slave. Got it?"

Wow. She may have been part immortal. But she was definitely one-hundred percent woman!

"As you wish, just stay close and do nothing without me." I really had nothing else to say to this very defiant and strong willed woman. She was obviously not going to lower herself under my authority. In a sense I could respect that, but damn she was cocky!

As I turned to continue down the sidewalk I heard her whisper, "Men!"

I knew this one would be difficult. She was her own being with her own will and I knew that it would not be easy to keep her out of trouble. She would be more likely to dive head first into a situation rather than think about the repercussions of her actions. Her stubborn nature could be dangerous. Nonetheless, I made a secret vow at that moment to protect her and guide her as best as I could. It wouldn't be easy working with a woman. It never had been for any species of male. Be it a human, animal, angel, or demon; females always seemed to know where in our crotch regions to grab and twist hard enough to dominate us.

While mortal men liked to congregate and brag about the number of women they had seduced, we vampires preferred to brag about the number of scum bag necks we had drained in a single night. I had often wondered what the female immortals discussed among themselves. The number of men that had fallen under their spells?

As we continued down the side of the street, I couldn't help but be aghast at Thia's attire. It was obviously not modern American and would certainly not be modern English when we arrived there. Most of us preferred to dress like everyone else around us, though I did fancy the long coat, top hat, and cane movies would always portray us with. I knew we needed to blend in. I was in my mid-twenties according to human years, so I wanted to maintain the appearance of such. But deciding which group I belonged to was rather difficult. I lived in the city so I tried to dress more like urban punk. There were so many of those running around here that no one paid them any attention.

It was the perfect cover. I also had to pretend that I couldn't smell the blood flowing in everything with a heartbeat. It was tempting, to say the least. But we were forbidden to feast on just any human. It was a bum rule that I was sure to break at some point. I could usually smell a nephilim and a watcher a mile off. Their blood was thick and dark. My belly would literally flutter in hunger if I sensed one of them was near. We were allowed to feed from any of them if we had to, because we could not drain them and thus they wouldn't die. *Unlike these weak humans.*

Thia was far too obvious. She drew too much attention to herself. As we ventured down the sidewalk, passing many mortals along the way, I could feel their eyes all over us. Only no one was really looking at me. They had their eyes all over her. I could taste the lust of the men that passed by, their deepest desires nearly oozed out of their slobbering mouths.

"You may need to change up your appearance some, Thia dear."

She looked down at her long black medieval style dress and snapped, "What is wrong with the way I dress?"

I stopped and turned to her, my eyes quickly fixed on her

voluptuous bosom that peaked out from under a tight purple and black corset.

I gave her a smirk and pointed. "*That* is what's wrong. I turn to look at you, and your jolly rockets nearly jump up and slap me in the face! No offense Thia, but you look like a thirteenth century hooker."

Perhaps that wasn't exactly the right term to use because the next thing I recall seeing was her open hand against my face. *Yeah, that'll teach me!*

"How dare you! My attire has been approved by every ruling member of the order!"

I rubbed the stinging pain in my jaw. "Yeah, did you also not notice that the entire ruling body is male? Listen to me Thia, you have to blend in. Be less conspicuous. The less attention we draw to ourselves the safer we are."

As I spoke we passed in front of a sporting good's store. She must have known what I was thinking when I paused. She flashed me a disgusted look. "Oh, I don't think so!"

"It's perfect. No one would ever suspect that you are anything more than human." I completed my sentence with a smile, one to which she was not reciprocating.

"I wouldn't be caught dead in that!" she scoffed.

"That's the point, to not die. If you keep walking around in, well, In *that*… Someone is going to end you. Now come on. Let's get you changed into something less blood-sucking vampire and more lady-like."

She protested, but eventually gave in to my suggestion and we purchased something less attractive; a gray track suit. I convinced her to turn over her vamp tramp get-up to a homeless woman. I chuckled inside imagining the woman using it to turn a profit. I felt rather dirty about it.

One of the best parts about being immortal is unlimited fiat currency. We could get our hands on that meaningless garbage anywhere. It also helped that the order gave us an allowance every month. So purchasing at will had become an art form of ours. Though we rarely had need for mortal possessions, there were times that it was necessary for our cause. In this case it was two plane tickets to wonderfully dreary England; land of high up pretentious twats that seemed to enjoy their high position in the world. They were very stubborn and arrogant. I actually fit in quite nicely among them, though sometimes the very strong urge to chew a few of them up and spit them out was hard to control.

The Irish were a bit easier to converse with, though their tempers could really flare over a pint or seven. I was certain that somewhere in Thia's lineage was a scorned Irish woman that took out revenge on her drunken husband and everyone he had ever known. *Have I really befell to the weakness of stereotyping other cultures like the humans? I have to work on that.*

As we boarded Flight 777 to England, Thia seemed restless and a bit apprehensive. I knew that if I confronted her with my observation she would just become confrontational. The closer we came to take off, the more nervous she appeared to be. It was as if she had never flown before. I chuckled to myself foreseeing how the experience would be for her.

We settled into our seats and waited for what I liked to call the pre-flight game plan. The part where a young flight attendant gets up in front of all the passengers, goes through the safety plan on the what-ifs of flying; or in better terms: what to do if the plane suddenly begins to spiral out of control and began its rapid descent to the earth. It was entertaining to say the least, especially for the first time fliers who were already anxious enough without hearing the words, "In the unlikely event that the plane should go down."

And who knew that the seat cushions could be used as a flotation device? Very handy when flying over alligator infested swamps. Thia watched and listened with an ever growing look of horror on her face. I really did not understand her fear. I mean we were immortals. In the unlikely event that we did crash, we would likely be the only survivors.

Unless Billy Bob seated across from us was quick-thinking and tightly secured his cushion to his ass and floated to some uncharted island in the ocean somewhere.

I watched as the stranger attempted to figure out the

headphones offered by the airline to watch movies aired on the back of everyone's seats. *He's doomed.*

Finally, the roar of the engines gave way to the thought that we were about to take off. Thia tensed up even more as she listened to the heavy and intimidating winding of the engines. She gripped the arm rests with all her strength and for a moment, I was certain she would rip them right out of the seats.

"Ah, the sounds of jet engines. Quite soothing huh?" I smirked as I turned my head to mock her with a cheerful grin. She still gripped the armrests tightly. *She should be gripping the cushion, according to the flight attendant.*

"You're an asshole, you know it? We could have taken a boat instead. At the very least we should have waited for Belfore!" she growled at me.

"But it would have taken us days to get there instead of hours. As far as Belfore goes, he can find his own way to England." *Did she really just call me an asshole?*

She gave her best pouty look and leaned over to gaze out of the window.

Yeah, that's a great thing for someone with a fear of flying to do.

Instead of saying anything further, I waited for her reaction when the plane began to move. It was just as I thought it would be. Her eyes wide and fixed on the seat in front of her; as if she could pick it up and throw it using just her will to do so. Her hands still clutched the arm rests and all of a sudden, her complexion went from a furious shade of red to a very pale green. It did not go well with her gray track suit at all. And if she thought this was bad, I eagerly anticipated her reaction to landing.

We started down the runway faster and faster until we hit the right speed for takeoff. She did not look well at all. And I just could not wrap my head around her fear. Even if we went high into the air, did a loop and nosedived into the ground below, she would walk away unscathed. Still, it was entertaining nonetheless.

Finally, once we were in the air, I had to inquire about her obvious fear of flying. "Thia, is there any logical reason that you are afraid of flying?"

She glared at me, still somewhat pale and a bit flustered. Her reply was quick and rather jolted. "Scared of heights."

I chuckled. "Why? We're almost impossible to kill."

"I can still fear death can't I?"

I shook my head in disbelief. "Why fear that which cannot harm you? Unless of course we managed to crash into a field of silver tipped wooden stakes, your fears aren't justified."

She folded her arms and continued to stare at the seat in front of her.

"Just look out at the beauty of all that surrounds us." I went from asshole to bastard at that point because the moment she gazed out of the window and realized how high up we were, she fainted. *Well, at least this part of the flight will be pleasant for her.*

I wondered how this fearless and brave woman was so easily consumed by an unnatural fear. I had to remind myself she was just a rookie. She needed some strict training for sure.

Thia remained out for the remainder of the flight, which was soothing to my ears. I did not have to endure nine hours of "I am woman, hear me roar" from her lovely, yet painfully arrogant lips. The best was yet to come; British immigration.

We just looked like the sort they would immediately deport back to our homeland. Luckily for me I had friends in high places, or friends in immigration who had supplied me with all the necessary paperwork, including passports with fictional names on them. While in England, I would be Jack and Thia would be Jill. If anyone asked, we were not there to fetch a pail of water. My buddy in immigration found the name selections to be humorous. I just hoped that it wasn't too obvious they weren't our real identities.

We finally reached our destination. By then Thia was fully alert and still pissed off. She said absolutely nothing as we left the plane and headed in the direction of immigration. As we moved along with a suitcase each full of mortal possessions that we wouldn't likely need, but had in case we did, Thia seemed flustered; more so than she had been on our flight here.

"What is bugging you?"

She said nothing, but glared at me. I was amused by all this, but still a bit confused by her demeanor. She had insisted that she come with me, but all of a sudden seemed defiant about coming. It was as if someone had twisted her arm and forced her to come with me. I would have been happier flying solo, especially when paired with a woman. But she just had to tag along.

We approached the immigration line and, having been in this situation before, I knew what to expect. Thia, on the other hand, did not. I wanted to brief her on what to say so that we would get into the country.

"When they ask why we are here, say we are on vacation. If they ask where we will be staying at, you tell them all over the place, that we are seeing the sites here."

"I am no idiot you know. I think I could figure that out myself."

She sure seemed agitated for some reason, maybe jet lag. I really never figured out how vampires experience jet lag. Unless the sun was shining brightly into one of the large pane windows and started to melt my skin, I wasn't entirely concerned. Our flight over had taken place at night so I knew it was day time outside. This would give us an opportunity to look around and plan our next move.

There was so much to see in an airport. Restaurants; souvenir shops, great if you want that twelve inch Big Ben clock, and of course the people. Those were the most entertaining, especially if you happened upon a foreign couple who did not speak the language trying to figure out where the toilets were. It was a good thing the toilets have gender pictures over them.

Yes, the people. I love to watch them and all their mortal antics. They seem to have no clue of what is really going on around them. They have on blinders and are being corralled in one direction. It was pretty sad really. They could enjoy life more if they'd just break free and do their own thing. There was the business man who is away from his home and family to sell an idea given to him by his corporate masters to make them more money while not giving the man much of an income at all. Still, he feels compelled to slave away for such masters without question. The missionaries on their quest to win souls in countries that don't even believe in their god. And the tired and frustrated middle class couple that needs a break from their stressful lives and families so they travel to a foreign country where nothing is even remotely familiar or normal to them and thus leading them into more stress and anxiety. *I dare them to find a free toilet in this city; I know I've tried! Talk about corporatism! Take that America!*

Then there is my favorite among the mortals; the fussy spoiled children of these desperate, sad individuals who they so stupidly assumed their mini-human spawn would enjoy one second of the hustle and fuss and all the chaos associated with it. Their faces always say it all: HELP! Poor little depraved creatures. Sometimes I wanted to bite them just to relieve them of this needless insanity. Alas, that was forbidden.

I saw one parent tugging on her defiant child who obviously did not want to get on the commuter train, but who was forced to because the parent assumed it would be better than the overcrowded double decker bus that drove twice the speed limit and narrowly missed pedestrians who chose to walk in the streets instead of the sidewalks. Damn pedestrians. They always have the right away.

I actually enjoyed seeing such things, in a rather sick and twisted sense of humor kind of way.

At last, we reached the immigration line. I carefully observed a window high on the wall behind the immigration check point and cursed the prefect again for not booking a flight that would land at night.

The sun's rays struggled to pierce through the clouds outside and into the window. I grew nervous. I had to avoid the sunlight. Though it would not kill us, I knew that it would definitely give us away. The light would expose us for the monsters that we were, or the monsters society believed we were. Our immortal and perfect beings would be jeopardized. Thia hardly noticed the sunbeams and proceeded through the line. I followed close to her, ready to act at a moment's notice.

We would have to make a run for it if our covers were blown.

As we walked slowly forward, each person in line ahead of us being cleared entry into the country, I began to sweat nervously. We were getting closer to being fully exposed by the sun. I had to share my concerns with Thia and hopefully devise an immediate plan of action.

I neared the immigration officer and the light, with Thia in front of me. My heart was really pounding now; or my virtual heart as my real one had turned to dust the day I was born. Thia stepped forward with her papers in hand. I noticed a small beam of sunlight shining on her arm. No indication whatsoever that she even noticed. No burning, not even the magnifying of her monstrous identity; nothing! This concerned me greatly as I wondered how she was not even the slightest affected by it!

I paused, knowing that it was my turn to pass through immigration and hopefully into the country. Thia, who had been cleared, stood ahead and motioned for me to hurry up. Beads of sweat were now dripping from my forehead, an obvious indicator to the immigration officer that something wasn't right with me. To linger would blow my cover and to move forward would as well. I was faced with the difficult decision on how to expose my identity. I decided on the latter, as I may still get in without being overly exposed. Just as I stepped up to where the sunlight was beaming down, I noticed it quickly faded away. I looked up to the giant window overhead and noticed the sudden thick cloud cover. *Phew! Thank you miserable British weather!*

The immigration officer looked at me with a puzzled expression. "Are you okay, sir? You look ill."

"Yes, sir. I get air sick sometimes."

He nodded sagely at me, checked my documents, asked the usual questions and in return I gave the rehearsed reply that I always do. He waved me through, welcoming me to their fine country. *A fine country indeed.* Luckily he did not notice our ridiculous names. I did not want to linger in the line to explain that one in a way that he would believe me.

Thia was waiting for me with a look of concern on her face that seemed a hint of annoyance as well. "What was the hesitation about?"

I gave her my own look of inquiring to which she seemed doubly confused by. "As you obviously didn't notice, that huge window above the immigration desk also bore the beams of our doom in it, to which you seemed completely immune to. Your arm was brushed with sunlight, yet you were not fazed by it. I'm wondering how that is possible."

She suddenly appeared nervous and incapable of a reasonable explanation. "Well, I guess I didn't stand in it long enough for it to take effect. Unlike some people I know, I prefer to get in and get out and not fanny around."

Wow, her use of British slangs was pretty convincing. Still, I was not in the least bit convinced. Something was up with this young gal. And it was at that point that I became suspicious of her and knew that I could not trust her until I knew exactly what she was up to and where she had come from.

"I wasn't 'fannying around', as you put it. I was a bit nervous about passing through direct sunlight. In case you haven't noticed we are on a covert mission here and we have to be careful not to expose ourselves to the wrong sorts."

"I know why we are here. Do you?" She almost had a condescending tone to her voice.

Of course I knew why we were here! It was she who had decided to tag along with me. How could I not know the mission and she did?

As we proceeded down the wide hall area to the baggage claim, I became increasingly frustrated. "Thia, this is very important and we cannot afford to screw it up. Now either you are with me or you aren't, but no more games. Tell me what is going on with you."

She stopped with an angry expression on her face and exhaled a deep sigh. "Okay, Lafayette. Before I tell you about me you must understand my loyalty to the order and to this mission. Regardless of who I am or where I came from, I am as devoted to this cause as you are."

Something stirred inside of me, somewhat frightening and unsettling. "Thia? What do I need to know about?"

She sighed and took a seat on one of the benches that were positioned in random places all over the airport. She turned her gaze from me to the floor below her feet. She seemed apprehensive.

"I wasn't created as you were. I was not born of nephilim blood or even a vampire hybrid." She stopped and I noticed she nervously pinched and pulled at her fingers. I felt a knot rise in my throat and I knew that the news she was about to reveal would be something I would not like.

"Thia?" The tone of my voice shifted from being a bit annoyed with her to being genuinely afraid.

"Lafayette," She looked deep into my eyes, as if she were trying to reach a soul that was not there. "I am a watcher."

Her words echoed in my mind and for a moment I could not speak. All I could feel was betrayal and anger. I tried to open my mouth and mutter some phrases of disgust, but I couldn't. I was, for the moment, speechless.

"I betrayed that family long ago. I joined the Order of Spera to help you and others destroy the works of my people. For generations I have seen their destruction and how they have stolen the will of men and it has to end, once and for all. Or there won't be a world left for even our kind to live in."

She stared down, almost humiliated. I felt somewhat betrayed by the order. *How dare they send her with me?*

I knew it was too late to abort our mission, but how could I trust her? What if she were leading me into a trap? I felt nervous and uncertain about letting her know my plans. She could snitch! But, then again, she could be the spy that the prefect spoke of. At that point, I did not know who to trust. I just knew that I still had a mission and, despite all else, I would not turn back now.

CHAPTER TWO
The Hunt

Thia's revelation stirred me as we ventured out into the city that night. My mind weighed heavy with the burden of knowing that I was in the presence of a creature I had set out to destroy. Was she being truthful with me? Had she really betrayed her own kind to help us? These were not simple questions and I did not expect to receive any answers any time soon.

England was just as I had remembered it being; cold, damp and miserable. But I thanked the gods I hadn't been sent to Saudi Arabia. I felt sorry for the poor soul that was sent there and secretly hoped it was Belfore. He had disappeared shortly after he was instructed to go with Thia and I and neither of us knew of his whereabouts. *Arrogant little prick.*

Then the sympathy waned and stirred a bit of happiness in my head. Just thinking of him with his better-than-you attitude stuck in a place where he would certainly not fit in and, more importantly, stuck in the kingdom of the east with people with bigger egos than his.

A chill crept over the back of my neck that felt like shaky icy finger tips softly caressing my skin. I shivered a bit and Thia gave me a mocking grin.

"Too cold for you here, Lafayette?"

"Not at all, but that sudden chill gets me every time"

We crossed the Westminster Bridge and I paused to peer out across the river. So beautiful it was; calm, yet unsettling. The dim city lights cast eerie shadows on every object in sight. There weren't a lot of people out roaming around at this time of night. That was good, as I would have no humans to hinder my mission. I looked up at the clock tower; its hands almost aligned on the twelve. I waited for that moment when the bell would cry out from its tower prison, and hopefully scare the lights out of Thia. I was certain she had never experienced 'ole Ben before. I felt a warm tingle in the pit of my stomach just imagining her jumping in the air and rushing to grab on to anything that wouldn't let her fall.

And then the glorious moment I had waited for happened. The first bell chime struck loud and hard and Thia did indeed jump. *The bridge Thia, jump there.* I thought. But she did not grab onto some inanimate object. Instead, she grabbed on to me. She flew at me like a mad raven with arms out, she latched on to me like a baby and shook with fear.

"Um, Thia, what are you doing?"

I looked down at her tightly wrapped around my body, her arms over my neck and her legs around my waist. It was quite awkward. But more so for her when she realized what she was doing and quickly pushed away from me.

"What the hell was that?!"

"That was a clock tower."

"And you didn't feel the need to warn me that dreadful thing would do that?" She put her hand over her chest and continued to breath heavy.

I just smiled as I leaned over the side of the bridge and stared down at the black water below. "Thia, you must get a grip on yourself. There are far scarier things out there than an old clock tower."

She rolled her eyes, "And do those scary things bellow out in the night and terrify the hell out of whoever hears them?"

I chuckled. "If only we were that lucky, we wouldn't have to search for them."

Thia seemed really on edge for someone with her powers and skills. She seemed far too human in my opinion. Nonetheless, she was put on this mission for a reason, one I just couldn't understand. But surely the higher ups knew something I didn't. Oh, how I wished that moment she had jumped off the side of that bridge instead of attaching herself to me...

I wasn't sure how long we would have to linger in this place before we spotted some of the watchers. Parliament was crawling with their likes. Everyone from the MP's to the Lords had at least one watcher among them. The common person wouldn't be able to tell them apart from the rest of the corrupt officials. But I could. It was in their eyes. Humans had a soul and souls are impossible to hide. They shine through everyone's eyes, no matter how evil they are. But the watchers, the nephilim, and vampires have no souls and their eyes are as black as hatred on a cold winter night. Mine and Thia's included.

Thia rested against the side of the old worn down bridge and appeared to be in deep thought. I didn't want to question her because that would get her talking again and I really was not in the mood to listen to her. But alas, the silence was short lived.

"Lafayette, I'm sorry I wasn't honest with you about who I am. I understand if this causes a certain level of distrust. Just know that at the time I was not in a position to reveal my true identity. But I'm as dedicated to this mission as you are. I just have to be careful who sees me because if they find out I'm working for the Order they'll have my head."

I stood up straight and stared deeply into her eyes. If she wasn't sincere she was a master at deception. But somehow I could not believe she was being deceptive.

"Just stay focused on the mission. We have to snuff out these dirt bags soon so I can get the hell out of this country. I am hungry and there won't be a decent drop of blood to feed on here. These people don't like salt."

I laughed in my head, but it was obvious Thia didn't get it. Oh well. Give her a few days and she would realize the food here was as bland as a lot of the natives. I just hoped she wasn't a huge fan of ice tea. To put ice in tea here was almost criminal. My mind wandered through random thoughts about why I hated this place and I realized that it wasn't because of the people. I typically hated humans all over the world. I think I hated this place because of all the evil that saturated it. The leaders of this great land mass were either straight from the pits of Hell or they were enslaved to the ones who were. Every ounce of leadership here was tainted and I was certain we wouldn't have to look for very long to find those we had come to destroy.

As minutes ticked on and the clock tower started to bore Thia rather than scare her to death, I knew that it was time to move. I also knew I wouldn't venture far from this area. I could almost smell the wicked slime that oozed out all over the place.

"Come on. We need to find somewhere to camp for the night." I turned to walk away from her and she just stood with a puzzled look on her face. When I noticed she wasn't right on my heels, I turned back to face her.

"Camp, Lafayette? What about a hotel? We aren't in the dark ages anymore and I hear the accommodations here are lovely."

I rolled my eyes. If I somehow managed to fail this mission it wouldn't be because of those dangerous goons out there, but because this woman will surely drive me to the brink of suicide! As the old saying goes, she could make a train take a dirt road. She was very bity for a woman, and that is really telling. I had never met someone with such a big chip on her shoulder before. Being a watcher and having to betray one's own kind would be enough to make anyone bitter and resentful. But why did she seem to harbor all of those feelings against me? Why did she seem to hate me so much? I guess time would tell, or at least I hoped it would. Right now, I couldn't spend very long pondering those questions. We had to get somewhere for the night. I was tired and annoyed and hungry and in my delusional starved state, even Thia had started to look a little tasty. Some foods should really come with warning labels.

We decided to stay at a local bed and breakfast. I always loved these more than hotels. They seemed more personal and a lot warmer in terms of hospitality. A bit more pricey though, especially in a city such as this, but well worth it. Even the human food smelled quite lovely first thing in the morning. I woke to its aromas and, for a second, contemplated actually eating some. Not that human food could hurt me. It just wasn't filling. But it smelled so good that I knew resisting was pointless.

I inhaled deeply the strong scent of fresh brewed coffee. It smelled not like the cheap stuff most people would purchase in their local grocery store. This smelled expensive, perhaps one of those rare blends you have to pay top dollar for. That scent was mixed with what I believed to be apple turnovers and cinnamon rolls. My stomach growled and I realized how desperate for nourishment I had become.

Thia lay next to me in the bed. Looking at her sleep reminded me of an angel. So calm, so beautiful, so deadly. I was a bit cautious about sharing a bed with her, but it was the only bed and we had to pretend to be a young married couple. Normally they will just give you a smirk and a few first night wedding tips that you don't ask for and really don't care to hear from perfect strangers. We heard it all the previous night from a woman old enough to be my grandmother. And in vampire years, that is old!

I knew it was time for Thia to wake up so we could get going. I reached out with a pointed finger and poked her exposed arm. She didn't flinch. I poked her again and still nothing.

"Thia, *Thiiiiaaaaa*," I said as I poked her again. She snorted, but remained asleep with mouth wide open. I rolled my eyes. *Good God this woman is hard to wake!*

I decided the only way I could wake her was by being what she loved most: an asshole. I grabbed a pillow from the other side of the bed and smacked her hard in the face. In a startled and terrified state she sprang straight, up gasping for air. Then she looked at me, still holding the pillow and what came next wasn't expected nor prepared for. She gripped the pillow firmly in her hands, took a large swing and slammed it against my head. I was a bit dazed and shocked, as I had expected her fist instead. *Could it be possible that she is starting to warm up to me?*

Without hesitation, I grasped my pillow firmer and swung it hard against her shoulder. She fell over laughing, which was something I never heard her do before. It was actually the most precious sound I could ever imagine come from those bossy lips of hers.

That made me smile. As she gripped her pillow to swing, I quickly jumped on top of her to prevent another blow. I pinned her wrists down and straddled her to prevent her from moving. And that is when something else happened. Instead of fighting me or trying to smack me again, she just laid there and stared deeply into my eyes. I could not help but stare back into hers; so blue, so beautiful, so tempting.

I did not think about the awkwardness of the moment or what was really going on here. I felt something I hadn't felt in a very long time; the urge to be really close to another person. The little guy on my right shoulder scolded me while the little guy on the left encouraged me to go for it. I wasn't sure what *it* was but I was certain *it* involved me and Thia. As I came to my senses, I quickly moved off her and relocated to a spot on the bed farthest from her.

"Shall we pretend that didn't just happen?" I questioned in a bit of a nervous tone.

"Sure Lafayette, if that helps you to retain your macho image." When I looked back at her, she shot me a grin and a look I hadn't seen from her before. In my own demon form, I found her rather… well… seductive and beautiful. While at the same time, a complete and utter bitch. *Ugh, Lafayette. What is wrong with you?*

I didn't want to give any more thought to what had just happened. I grew nauseous that I had for a second wanted to do human things with her. *You have to pull yourself together Lafayette. You have a mission to complete. Damn women are always getting in our heads!*

As soon as I pulled myself away from a more human desire of intimacy, I realized that I had fell prey to another human desire; hunger. I knew that finding proper nourishment in broad daylight would be difficult, if not impossible, so a quick substitute would be the only option for now. I really hoped we could find one of those demons we had been sent here to hunt and destroy. I had planned to devour him or her like a starving wolf. In the meantime, a cinnamon danish would have to suffice.

"Thia, I don't know about you, but I am so hungry I could eat you."

We made our way down to the ground floor via the elevator. She shot me a sarcastic grin. "Well I am sorry I don't share those feelings. You don't really look appetizing to me."

She moved her gaze to my arms which were concealed by a full length coat. Then she pinched my arms and went on to say, "Skin and bones. That is all you are."

"Hey. I am not skin and bones. I'm... athletic."

She smirked and shook her head.

"Denial is the destroyer of all happiness."

"It isn't denial. I'm not skinny. And I think the correct phrase is *envy is the destruction of joy.*"

"Whatever. You will always be in denial, like you were this morning when you pretended that little incident didn't rouse you just a bit."

"I don't know what you're talking about." I once again tried to pretend I was clueless. She saw right through me.

"As you wish."

She refused to argue any further and I knew she was winning.

It was too late; I could no longer focus on the task at hand because I reveled in the thought of our physical encounter. I needed something to shake me out of my hypnosis and get me back on track. The combination of starving and feeling mentally exhausted did not help matters. I just wanted to be back home in the comfort of my own man cave.

The elevator doors opened, revealing an older man with this strange empty expression on his face standing before us. He was dressed in a dark blue suit. Sagging skin hung loosely on his skull and his white hair was combed neatly to one side.

He looked into my eyes and that was when I noticed this was no human at all. This was a creature of the night. His intentions towards us appeared on his face in the form of a twisted grin.

I grabbed Thia's hand and we began to run. We hurried down the hallway and I flung the exit door open. We fled with our lives; me still holding on to her hand. I led her into an alleyway where we slumped down behind some wooden crates that were stacked up beside one of the doors. We both tried to catch our breath. I realized that somehow our covers had been blown and they knew we were here.

She gasped and leaned over, placing her hands on her knees

and panting hard. "Lafayette, who was that?"

"I was about to ask you the same question."

"I don't know who that was! Is he gone?"

I looked over the crates and saw the mysterious figure standing in the alley entrance. He was looking in the opposite direction. It was clear that he did not know where we were.

I sat down behind the crates and pulled her closer to me.

"He is at the alley entrance. This is bad Thia. They know we are here. How did they know?"

She looked as confused as I was and as much as I wanted to blame her, I really couldn't. Perhaps the watchers had kept a closer watch on her than I had considered. Maybe they were using her as bait. I wasn't sure what the scenario was but it concerned me that instead of being the hunters, we had now become the hunted.

We sat still and quiet, so as to not draw any attention to ourselves. My stomach was really growling at this point and the smell of the nearby bakery was overwhelming for me. I held Thia in my arms closely, like a mother wolf guarding her cub. Her arm was wrapped around my waist. Neither of us concerned ourselves with how awkward it would have felt had we not been hiding for our lives.

I slowly and quietly leaned forward, just slightly, until I could barely see beyond the crates. The demon was gone. With a sigh of relief, I relaxed my posture and my grip on Thia.

"I believe he's gone." I stood slowly and reached out to take her hand. Pulling her up, she stood very close to me and diverted her gaze to the ground. She gently touched my hand then peered back up at me; not saying a thing but letting me know in a non-verbal way how thankful she was for me being there with her. My hardcore little demon was starting to soften up. I wasn't sure I liked this new Thia. She was far less bitchy this way though.

"Let's go. Quickly. He may still be nearby." I looked all around as we carefully exited the alleyway. I looked from left to right and seeing no one but the usual passersby, we continued on down the concrete sidewalk, still looking over my shoulder for a man that did not fit with the crowd.

I was relieved that the day was overcast. The absence of sun light would conceal our identities, at least to the humans. Had the sun been beaming down on us, we would have been forced to hide out somewhere until it clouded up, or until the sun began to set. This was one of the few things I loved about this place; almost always overcast.

It was so cold outside that I almost wanted to snuggle up with Thia. Then I realized what an absurd idea that was. I was doing everything possible to not think about what happened back in our room. I could not allow emotions to cloud my judgment right now. I needed to stay alert and focused, now more than ever, if we were to survive.

But alas, my hunger pangs were beginning to distract me from anything else and I knew we needed to eat soon. For blood suckers such as myself who are in need of a quick fix without drawing attention to ourselves, the most undercooked beef was the best option. It wasn't as filling as the blood of humans or other demons, but it would suffice for a time.

We quickly darted through the doors of a restaurant which I knew served meat. I could smell the blood boiling in the ovens from where we stood outside. This was not just about getting a quick snack. It was also a way for us to hide while observing our surroundings. We chose a table near a large window so that we could keep a look out. Since the sun was hidden away by thick gray clouds, for the moment I wasn't in fear of being exposed. Thia seemed a bit unsettled, more than she had been since arriving here. But she was quiet about it.

The waiter quickly approached us and began to ramble on about their special of the day. I really didn't want to listen to his senseless banter.

"A glass of water for each of us and two of the biggest and rarest steaks you can cook. Okay?" I smiled as I doled out my most pleasant tone and handed back the menus.

He appeared insulted, as if preventing him from spending five minutes recommending wines that neither of us would drink had really ruined his day. He nodded and walked away.

Thia stared out of the window and said nothing.

I watched her as her eyes darted nervously back and forth monitoring the street. "There will be more like him you know. The closer we get to them, the more they will send. We can't hide forever."

She sighed and peered down at her hands, which were clasped together in her lap. "It's my fault," she mumbled. I was confused by her statement and pressed her for more information.

"Thia, how is it your fault?"

She looked up at me and rolled her eyes. She brought her hands up and propped her chin in her palms. "Because they have been after me for years. I'm sure they hoped I would lead them straight to your order, or to other organizations like yours that are scattered all over the world. I should have seen this and been more careful."

I reached across the table and took her hands in mine. Her expression told me that she had thought of our little encounter earlier that day. But she seemed less stressed when I touched her. As if my energy calmed and soothed her. If that were the case, it had been worth a bit of humiliation to show her that she could trust me.

"Thia, you can't blame yourself. They'd track me down with or without your help. We just have to work together to make sure that we move in on them first. I know it's going to be dangerous. I know we may get hurt or worse, killed. But this is something we have to do."

I pointed out the window. "Look outside. Do you see all of the buildings, the concrete... the people? They're destroying their world and they don't even seem to notice or care. They have given up one of their most valuable qualities: humanity. They've been turned into mindless drones incapable of even thinking for themselves anymore. And this is because the ones we are hunting have slowly and cleverly destroyed all that they once held dear. Humans are dying a slow decay and, to them, it's normal. Death is something they expect and look forward to because it releases them from the clutches of their invisible masters. That is why we are here, Thia. This is our mission: to destroy those evil life sucking monsters and restore humanity to what they were created to be."

Thia sighed in agreement, but still seemed somewhat troubled.

After nearly twenty minutes the waiter brought us two plates of the bloodiest steaks I had ever seen. He set them down in front of us and I almost licked my entire face looking at the delicious bloody flesh.

Normally I wasn't a meat eater, just a blood sucker. But in order to conceal what we were, we would have to devour the entire thing. Thia did not seem bothered by this fact and dug right in like she was starving... and using her hands instead of utensils!

"Thia, use a damn fork woman! We aren't dogs!" I looked around and noticed there were many eyes on us, and this was not what I had wanted.

She peered up from her steak, which she grasped in both hands and had the flesh to her lips licking the blood that dripped from it. When she realized how much attention she had on her, she came up with a clever plan to satisfy the onlookers.

"I am so sorry my love. It has been days since I feasted on such delicious food." She spouted in a perfect Brazilian accent. This threw off onlookers and gave them the impression that she was a refugee or something and starved. She lowered the meat and winked at me as the onlookers slowly went back to their own meals, ignoring Thia.

I leaned in and with a grin. I whispered, "Well played Thia."

She just smiled and continued eating, this time without so many eyes on her.

"Oh my goodness! This is so good!" A soft moan escaped her as she continued to devour the flesh.

The steaks were just what we needed for now. We would have to find proper food later, but that would at least keep us going for some time.

As we ascended from the restaurant some time later, I noticed that the clouds were starting to clear out a bit. We would need to find shelter for the time being, so that we would not be exposed. Well, so that I wouldn't be exposed. Thia was not affected by the sun. But I could still see the blackness of her non-existent soul. That's something she could not conceal. At least from those with a keen eye to see who she was inside.

As we stood just on the outside of the restaurant I scanned the faces of everyone around me, as if I were a paranoid fugitive planning an emergency escape route. No one appeared suspicious, at least not instantly. They all appeared to be busy and in a hurry which worked to our advantage. While they were hustling past me to get to wherever they were going, I would hustle with them and just be a part of the crowd, decreasing my chances of standing out.

The sun had begun to beam through the thinning clouds which made me very anxious. I took Thia's hand in mine and tugged on her as I began my brisk stride down the side walk towards a more shaded area, which happened to be an alley way. I didn't mind the alleys, but Thia seemed nervous by them. At least there we stood a chance of not being spotted and maybe having more time to come up with a plan. They were on to us, and it was only a matter of time before they found us again.

She said nothing as she followed closely to me. Our shoulders bumped into the shoulders of others and no one had time to say "pardon me." We weren't trying to be rude. We just wanted to get out of there quickly. As I tried to hurry, fearing the sun's exposure, Thia stumbled over her own feet and nearly hit the ground. I stopped abruptly to help her regain her footing and we continued quickly to the alley.

"Lafayette, slow down! I can't walk that fast!" She scolded me, her voice winded and frustrated.

I glanced back at her and slowed my pace a bit. "Thia the sun is coming out. We have to get somewhere safe. We need to hurry!"

I tried not to sound angry, but my tone came out as such. As we proceeded, I sensed a presence that made me very uneasy. This prompted me to pick up the pace once again. Thia, realizing that something wasn't right, tried to keep up. My heart began to pound an unstable rhythm and my palms became sticky with perspiration. It was getting closer, I could feel its eyes on us and waiting for an opportunity to strike. I was not entirely sure what we were up against, as I had yet to see it. But it was obvious to me that it did not fear attacking us in broad daylight in front of witnesses. Whatever it was, it was certain that no human would be able to stop it.

I looked to my left, tall towering buildings made of granite stone shielded a few of the sun's rays from us. To my right were a few not so tall shops of various types. A mobile phone shop with flashing lights in its large smudged up windows, a bakery with a mixture of sweet scents that made me nauseous to inhale, a video game store where a bunch of teenagers loitered the area surrounding the shop, and a place to go to when inquiring about residential housing in the area. All of these pointless and expensive things just to pacify the humans. All I craved at this moment was to escape whatever was quickly gaining on us.

We reached the entrance to a small, narrow alley and quickly ran towards the end, which had no outlet. If the thing tailing us saw us retreat here, we would have no escape. We stood at the end, a tall chain link fence blocking our escape, and looked in every direction.

"Lafayette, where is it?"

I looked up and down the brick walls of the surrounding buildings. They were damp with condensation and a bit moldy. The ground beneath our feet was paved in worn down bricks, some were missing, some were displaced, and small puddles of water had formed in the absence of the bricks. My skin was crawling with fear, I knew that it was close.

"We have to hide. It's coming!" I whispered as my eyes fearfully darted in all directions.

Thia clung to me and I could feel her body tremble with fear. I was not sure if she had sensed the same being that I had, or if she was just reacting to my own fear.

Before either of us had time to react, we were violently pulled into one of the doors in the alley. I prepared to fight as we regained our footing and watched the door shut to the outside.

46

The room was rather dark with only a candle illuminating very small areas at a time. The figure that had grabbed us stood still, pressing his ear to the door. He said nothing and we were frozen with fear once again and I debated if we should run or just try to talk our way out of this.

The figure before us slowly backed up, without facing us. "I believe it is gone. But best you stay here until we can be certain. Here, you are safe."

I was puzzled, as I knew Thia was too. *Did he just save us? Who was he?* The figure turned to face us. The dim glow of the candle lit his withered old face in an orange glow.

"*You!*" It was the old man we had encountered in the hotel lobby earlier.

"Yes. I am Valice or if you prefer my human name, Vick. You run quite fast there Lafayette. I was certain Thia would slow you down."

At this point, I was really confused. The old man walked past us and retrieved the candle from the table. He lit two more he pulled from his pocket. Thia and I just stood in disbelief. He was a demon, I saw it in his eyes. Yet he had saved us.

I mentally noted how he was easily able to afford a suit, but not electricity. Though I had to admit, the candles were a nice touch for the dank lil' shanty.

"Who are you and why are you following us?" Thia raised her voice just slightly over a whisper.

I nudged Thia, "He is Valice, aka; Vick." My tone was mocking and obviously noted by Vick who raised a brow at me.

He placed the freshly lit candles on the table and motioned for us to sit, which we reluctantly obliged.

"As I said, I am Valice. And like you Thia, I am one of the original watchers. And I also betrayed the order ages ago."

We listened attentively as he took a seat across from us. He turned his gaze to me. I was able to see straight into his eyes.

They were cold and hard, like a block of ice resting solitary in a dark frozen cave. He did not trust me, this much I could tell. It wasn't apparent why.

"The watchers are on to you, but they are not the only ones."

"We know that. They obviously know that we are out to kill them and want to stop us."

Valice's eyes widened for a moment, seemingly annoyed with my arrogance.

"The order sent you here, blindly following orders to kill and they gave you no idea as to how you can go about destroying creatures that can't be killed. I don't think either of you really know why you are here."

"We are here to kill the watchers and restore order between the gods and mankind," I reiterated.

The room grew silent except for a breeze that whistled through the cracks of the old house.

"How typical of the order to send their army into battle and not even train or instruct them on how to defeat the enemy. They surely have not changed tactics over the centuries."

"So how do we kill them?" Thia's voice was weak.

Valice peered at her over the flicker of the candle before him.

"Thia, watchers have been around since before this planet was born. What makes you so certain that you could defeat them even if you wanted to?"

As much as I didn't want to admit it, he was right. We had no idea how to defeat the watchers. But they had threw us out into the fight nonetheless.

"The order did not inform you of how to kill them because you can't, not on your own." Vick's nostrils flared at the mention of the watchers and death, as if he were thinking of his own demise.

"Then why are we here?" I asked.

Vick cleared his throat and paused for a minute. "The order sent you here on a suicide mission."

Vick's tone was so matter of fact like that I feared challenging him.

"Wha—?" Thia asked with a look of shock on her face.

"The head of the order is known by many names. And he has been around longer than all of the angels in the heavens and on Earth. He infiltrated the vampires long ago to gather intel and secretly plan his next course of action."

"Which is?" I asked.

"Vampires are a cursed breed, but not fully cursed. You have the immortality of a watcher. But you have the compassion and forgiving nature of the humans. Only you can find what they are truly looking for: the Tree of Life."

For a moment I wanted to laugh. But he seemed so serious, which made me more uncomfortable.

"The Tree of Life. Really?" Thia pondered out loud.

"When the gods kicked the leader of the watchers out of Heaven and cast him upon Earth, he put a gateway here so that demons could travel back and forth to other realms; which they have been doing since the beginning. But the one place they long to return to is the Tree of Life. No one without a soul may pass through the portal leading to it. I know that you've been told as vampires you have no souls. But from the moment you were birthed by your human mothers and drew your first breath, a soul entered into your bodies. It became your conscience, your empathy, and everything that is human about you. While you still possess certain demon qualities, you do in fact have a soul. Not like your average human, but one such as all celestial beings possess."

I was in shock. For all of my years existing on this miserable planet I felt that I was a soul-less monster and nothing more.

"You… have a soul? Lafayette?" Thia leaned in closer to me, sniffing as if I suddenly had a new scent. I grew annoyed with her and pushed her away from me.

"This can't be. I am a monster. I've always been a monster," I responded somewhat confused and feeling a bit betrayed.

"Lafayette, I tell you this because it's very important for you to know this secret and use it to your advantage; because the watchers' want to use it too. Since the beginning of time, they had meticulously planned an attack on the human species, to rid this world of all that can gain access to the Tree of Life and immortal lives in Heaven. They have been jealous of the humans since they were created and have longed for nothing more than to destroy them."

He stared at me a moment before continuing. "It is your immortality that keeps you alive. But it is your human side that gives you the passion and drive to protect the humans and to save them from the watchers."

I really could not figure out where he was going with this. He still hadn't answered my questions. He had mentioned 'suicide mission' but hadn't yet explained that. Vick would not let me silently question for long.

"Lafayette, there is a war brewing; one that could potentially eliminate most all of the humans on earth. Those remaining would be enslaved by these watchers and their souls devoured so that they can pass through the portal at the Tree of Life, gain entrance into Heaven where they plan to over throw the gods, and claim that kingdom for themselves. With all humans wiped out, their power grows stronger. This war will be unlike any in the history of mankind. Only a demon with the compassion and drive of a human can stop it."

"How?!" I wanted to skip all the details and just get right to the point; like a child reading a story who doesn't want to read the middle to find out what happens and skips to the last page.

"You're not going to be able to defeat the watchers, not so easily. But you can begin to take out their followers, those who do their bidding without a question or a blink. Unfortunately for you, the ones you need to destroy are also the same ones you have to protect."

"Humans!" Thia announced, with a sigh of frustration and a look of bewilderment.

"Yes. The watchers have many humans working for them to carry out this master plan of total destruction and death. These humans don't realize who they are working for. They are, in a sense, hypnotized. But nonetheless, they are working directly for the watchers and unless you find and remove them, the watchers will grow stronger every day."

"So what happens *if* we do destroy all of these... sheep? How then do we destroy the watchers?" I asked.

Vick heaved a rather unpleasant sigh and gave us both a look over.

"I really do not know how."

This wasn't what we wanted to hear at all. We had come so far yet not far enough and we still had so many unanswered questions.

"The order had wagered that neither of you would survive this mission. But now that you know that there is a snake among them, you cannot communicate with them ever again or trust a word that comes from them. There are others like you. But I share this information with only you. Take it, heed it, and be on your guard."

He leaned back in his chair, eyes staring into mine when next he spoke. "From now on, disregard all previous orders from the fools and do only as I say. If you want to live and restore humanity to what it once was, you must listen to me and me only."

"How do we know we can trust you?" Thia asked abruptly.

Vick smiled. "I don't expect you to, not yet. But in time you will see that I am on your side; the side of the humans and I want this war to end. It has been going on for so long and I am tired. Without a human soul, I can't just rest in peace in a meadow somewhere and wake up in the heavens surrounded by all of my friends and loved ones. The watcher life is a sad and lonely. Alas, it is my destiny."

There was a slight change in his tone; from a strong and courageous sounding man to a tired and worn out old man. It's like he was ready for his earthly life to end and another to begin somewhere else in another realm.

"You are mankind's only hope. Once you begin to remove the foundation of a building, eventually it will collapse. Remove it stone by stone, it becomes weak and unstable. That is what you must do to the watchers. And in the end, when they are weak and fragile, you will know how to completely destroy them."

Suddenly our mission became a lot easier, but a lot scarier. Taking out humans was easy. They were extremely vulnerable.

But to do so without our identities being broadcast all over the world would be difficult. If we just rushed in and started killing, we would be discovered, our covers blown, and mission failed. We had to figure out a way for these humans to just self-destruct. And at the moment, I did not have a plan.

"Lafayette, I know what it is you wonder and I can only assure you that if you do this, mankind stands a chance. You have to stop the war that is coming. If this means you lose your life in the process, then that is the will of the gods."

"Yeah speaking of them, why don't they just destroy the watchers? Why do we have to go through all of this when the gods could just smite them down or something?" I asked.

"Lafayette, you aren't a parent... not yet at least. But if you were a parent, wouldn't you find it hard to harm your own child? That is what the watchers are. They are the gods' first children, if you will. They had hoped that the watchers, vampires, and humans would resolve this on their own without intervention. They know what is coming. And they have faith in you and all of the vampires that your human sides will prevail. They can't kill this evil. But you can."

"So I guess this is it. We have to destroy the bad humans working for the asshole watchers, which you and Thia are but you are both good and somehow that is supposed to comfort and reassure me so that I can complete this mission?"

"Something like that," Vick ended with a sarcastic grin.

"Great, I feel loads better now."

"Hurry now. The one that followed you is close. He is a demon that is neither watcher nor vampire, something worse. You must leave this place at once. Find somewhere safe to hide while you search for the humans. And when you find them..." He paused and looked at us, "Don't be so obvious about who you are. The less you leave behind in way of evidence the better. Now go!"

CHAPTER THREE
Reunion

Lee was someone that I had met many years back when we were both kids. He was an overweight boy who was teased and bullied by his peers. I stood up for him a few times and we became close friends. Even though he was a human, he was a good kid.

The day my true identity was revealed to him was a day I will never forget. We were teens playing football in the park, the sky overcast and gray, when Lee's bullies approached us.

"Hey look, it's the walrus and the weirdo." Taunted one of the kids, causing the other three to burst into laughter.

I grabbed Lee's arm and gave him a nudge.

"Let's get out of here." I said in a low voice.

Lee stood frozen in fear, unable to move. The bullies surrounded us and it was in that moment I realized we were trapped. The only way out was to fight. Something I knew Lee couldn't do and I did not want to for fear of being exposed.

As the boys laughed and mocked us, I could smell the blood pumping through their veins. It excited me and my nostrils flared at the strong iron stench. I fought hard to overcome the desires in my head but the smell of their warm blood was starting to get to me.

The leader of the gang shoved Lee, causing him to lose his balance and fall helplessly to the ground. He landed on his stomach and I could hear the gasp of air leave his mouth.

The boys cheered and laughed as I scrambled to help my friend up. Just as I bent down I felt a strong, hard kick in my back that sent me tumbling over Lee and landing face down in the dirt. I rolled quickly onto my back. One of the kids quickly straddled me and pinned me down. He began to pound his fist into my face. With each blow, I could feel my flesh rip, the blood spattered on the kid's shirt and my anger began to mount in an evil aggression. I could no longer control the rage that had built up inside of me.

As the other kids continued to cheer and mock us, Lee tried to crawl away unnoticed, but failed. One of the other kids kicked him, knocking him back down on the ground.

As the blows to my face continued, the kid's hand slammed against my teeth puncturing his flesh. From there on, everything moved in slow motion as he withdrew his hand and looked at the wound that had now begun to bleed. And then, drops of his warm blood fell onto my lips, instantly transforming me into the demon that I had tried to hide my entire life.

My body began to tremble, sweat beaded up on my forehead, and my eyes turned completely black. A power from within took over with such force that in an instant, the kid was hurling into the air. As he was launched backwards his hand grabbed onto a necklace that hung around my neck, breaking the chain with violent force.

The pendant was given to me as a small child to control my demonic tendencies. As I would mature, I would learn to control them on my own. But for now, I was neither mature enough nor strong enough to harness the demon inside of me. The second it was ripped from me, I lost all control over myself. I sprung to my feet and began to violently throw each and every kid that had stood around mocking us. I wanted to devour them. I wanted to taste their delicious, warm blood and to make them suffer.

As each kid landed on the ground in a hard thud, I ignored their whines and groans of agony and rushed to the leader who lay still on the ground in fear, with my necklace still clutched in his palm. His eyes were wide as he stared at me with absolute fear.

"What the hell are you?" He gasped.

I knelt down, grabbed his hand, and ripped my necklace from his bloodied hands. As I did I inhaled deeply the sweet scent of his blood.

I glared into his eyes and said, "I am your worst nightmare."

I jumped to my feet and watched as all the bullies fled in fear, shouting obscenities back at us, as if it was of any threat to me.

I walked over to Lee. He was still on the ground in a state of shock and fear. I extended my hand to him. He let out a blood curdling scream. I quickly knelt beside him and scooped him up into my arms *and pulled him close to me.*

"Shh. I'm not going to hurt you. You're my friend." I gently stroked his hair and felt his rapid breathing began to slow. His body relaxed and I leaned away from him.

I looked into his eyes. They reflected fear, uncertainty, and a sense of betrayal and distrust.

"You… your face… it…" His eyes were wide and terrified.

I pulled him to me with a gentle hug to reassure him that even though I may look like a monster, I really wasn't. When provoked, anyone could become the thing that they feared most.

"It's something I hoped you'd never see. It's a curse handed down to me by my father. But I won't hurt you. You're my only friend."

Lee turned his gaze away from me and to the ground below and his body relaxed even more.

"Please promise me that you will never tell anyone."

"What about those kids? They saw you too."

I thought for a moment of how I would explain what they saw while convincing them that it was only an illusion.

"I'll just tell them it was a trick, to scare them off." Lee looked back up at me and we both smiled. He vowed that he would never tell my secret, to be forever in my debt, and that if I ever needed him to just call on him.

He picked up the phone on the third ring. I could hear his lips smacking as he chewed on something crunchy.

"Lafayette, long time no… well, anything really. Where have you been man?"

"Hey buddy. Um… I really need your help. And anyone that you trust that can help, I need them too."

"Hmm, by the tone in your voice, it sounds to me like you have gotten yourself into some trouble. What did you do this time? Leave DNA evidence after a midnight snack? Wait, do vampires have DNA?"

"Lee listen, this is important and… wait, what? Yes, we have

DNA. I am half-human you asshole."

"I'm just saying you know. Not that I know much about vampires except you don't fit the Hollywood norm."

"Do you still have contact with that computer geek friend of yours, what was his name? Harold? Hank?"

"Heratio?"

"Yeah that guy. You still hacking government databases with him?"

"Lafayette! This is an open line man. You can't say shit like that!"

"Sorry. You know I am messing with you. But seriously, I need your help. Also that friend of yours that used to do the underground smut stuff that knows a little about every dirty politician in the world."

I could hear Lee shifting his weight over the phone.

"This sounds serious man. What's going on?"

"How fast can you get to London?"

"Hmm... well, it's about a nine hour flight from New York, I am in LA—."

"I will book you on the next flight out of LAX. I need you to get your geek pal and pervert and bring them too. I will wire you over the money now. Go get those tickets and meet me in London. It's urgent man. I will fill you in on the details when you get here. Okay?"

For a moment I heard more chewing, a lot slower this time though. I hated indecisiveness. "I promise, this is a mission that is going to tickle that crazy mind of yours."

"All right, all right. Let me make some phone calls and I will get back to you. Whatever this is, it sounds good and I want in on it. So yeah, keep your phone close. Stay out of sunlight and churches."

I rolled my eyes at his vampire humor. He tried to be funny, but it sounded more insulting. Since he was my closest friend, I just let it slide.

"You really are an idiot you know?" I reminded him.

"Yeah I know. But it's *you* calling on *me* for help. "

He laughed and I heard him take a sip from his beverage.

Then he released a disgusting sounding burp.

"Great. Call me back as soon as you can. Thia and I will be on stand-by until I hear something from you."

"Thia? Is she that pretty looking Asian chick you were shacking up with the last time I saw you?"

"No. That was breakfast."

"Oh… That is just so not funny man! You killed that cute Asian girl?"

"No. I mean really she was breakfast."

"Ah. Dirty man." He chuckled.

"You really didn't think we vampires live a life of celibacy did you?"

"I don't know. Don't care to know; too much info for me. It's just kinda' gross. So yeah. Let me call around. I will get back to you."

I hung up. Thia stood oddly close to me, as if she were eaves dropping on my conversation.

"Who was breakfast?"

"Oh, that? It's nothing. Lee is just being a condescending idiot."

"Some Asian chick?"

I looked at her in disbelief.

"Wow your hearing is excellent and your keen sense of butting into a private conversation is remarkable. For your information it's a girl I used to date."

"Vampires date?" Thia asked with a puzzled look on her face. I rolled my eyes and sighed.

"Okay are there any more vampire clichés you'd like to drill me about? Like does silver kill me? Only if it punctures my heart but a copper bullet can do the same. Does sun light turn me onto a pile of ash? Only if I forget to wear my SPF 70. What else Thia? Of course we vampires date. We also have sex and have children which we were doing until the order put a stop to it."

"Okay, okay. Touchy tonight?"

"No, I just don't like being bombarded with questions about who I have slept with. While we are on it, Thia, you're technically an angel. Do angels have hormones? Besides the estrogen that makes them insufferable bitches?"

She could tell by my tone that I didn't like this line of questioning although she seemed more than willing to answer my own questions.

"Well yeah. Of course angels fall in love and do all those things. How do you think your kind came to be? I was just asking. I'm in on this too and I didn't want old baggage to come up and bite us in the ass, get it?"

I turned away from her and sighed, feeling a bit embarrassed now at how I had blown up at her. She did have a right to know who I was bringing in on this mission who weren't immortals.

"The Asian girl, her name was Yuri. I met her in high school soon after I met Lee. Her family settled in the states when she was a baby and she didn't have a lot of friends. She hung out with me and Lee and a couple of other friends. We started seeing each other regularly outside of our circle of friends and just became really close.'

"Wow. I didn't know you were capable of that sort of thing." Thia huffed and folded her arms in front of her. *Was she jealous?*

"I am capable of a lot of things, Thia. Being a vampire doesn't automatically make me an uncaring bastard. I may have my father's demon side. But I also inherited my mother's caring human side. I feel love, hate, anger, pride and all the emotions any other human feels. I just have a better way of hiding it so that people like you think I am a total dick. I'm really not. And if you took two seconds to just understand me and not draw your own shady conclusions, you would see that."

"I don't know what conclusions to draw. You are a mystery. I know absolutely nothing about you other than what you have told me standing here. Which, it's cold out here. I hate London so much. You haven't showed much emotion at all which only forces me to think you don't feel any. You don't have a beating heart in that chest of yours, do you?"

I faced her and looked directly into her eyes. Even in the cold night air, I could see the clarity in her pupils and understood perfectly what she was trying to say to me. I took off my coat and draped it over her shoulders. She looked down, ran her fingers across the black soft fibers and tilted her head somewhat to glance up at me.

"I have a heart. It isn't like that of a human. But it's there. And it hurts just the same when words such as yours fly out without any consideration."

She said nothing as she continued to look at me and listen to me pouring out my cold dead soul in the most pathetic tone ever. I couldn't believe I was allowing her to see this side of me. Very few people had ever seen it. I built up my bad boy image so long ago that I had almost forgotten my softer side.

"I'm sorry, Lafayette. You're just such a difficult person to understand. You live the life of a demon yet you have a moral side to you that I just don't understand. How did such a creature like you even survive this long? A demon thrives off hurting others and being destructive."

I drew her close to me and stared deeply into her eyes. She gasped softly at my abrupt force on her body and said nothing.

"I survived because I was meant to. I am a demon of sorts. I am also human. My heart, while nothing like a humans, beats, bleeds, aches, and longs for the love and affection of another."

I held her close to me a bit firmly, making her rather nervous but curious as to where this would lead to. "It is my morality and compassion for these bleeding humans that will end the wars and suffering on this entire planet and bring about a peace that was sought after since the beginning of creation. The gods will recognize my loyalty not only to their kind but to their creation as well and perhaps they will reward me with something I have never had and have always longed for."

"What's that?' Thia asked softly, still gazing into my eyes.

I drew her even closer to where her breath could be felt on my lips, "A human soul."

Without any further hesitation, I pressed my lips onto hers for a soft and gentle kiss. I felt her gasp and for a moment she held on to me. Her lips were soft and moist but quivered anxiously. But then she pulled away from my grip and turned away.

I did not know what to think. Was she angry at me? Did she

like it? She had to have liked it. I knew she had wanted to do that since the day we left base. She gave off that vibe. But she was a tough one and did not let on to any affectionate thoughts or actions; except that pillow fight in the hotel. Until now, that was as close as we had gotten.

"Thia? Are you okay?"

She still had her back to me and I could see her raise her hands to her lips, as if she could not completely acknowledge what had just taken place.

I slowly approached her from behind and slid my arms around her waist. She flinched ever so slightly. But for once, she didn't completely pull away from me.

"It's just... that was so sudden. I wasn't expecting it."

I turned her facing me, looked deeply into her eyes and smiled. "I am not the heartless beast you think I am."

"I never said you were anything of the sort. I... shit! I don't even know what I was going to say. You have my head all crazy now!"

I chuckled and pressed my finger to her lips in a teasing way, although I really did want her to just shut up. Her lips were beautiful when pressed to mine. But when they were doing anything else besides kissing me and breathing, they became quite annoying.

"Let's go find somewhere to sleep for the night and wait for Lee to call me back, okay?"

For the first time since we began our journey together, Thia seemed really apprehensive about even the thought of us sharing a room together. I rather enjoyed this side of her. It was a pleasant change from the bitchy Thia I started out with. She was still a bitch, but one that I found myself strangely attracted to.

That night, I tossed and turned, struggling to sleep. Another myth about vampires, we do sleep. Our bodies get tired like anyone else and, contrary to belief, we don't sleep in coffins. I tend to be claustrophobic so that would never work for me. Plus, who buries a vampire in a coffin? If we do turn to ash when silver pierces our hearts, or when the sun hits us, what's left to bury? Oh the vampire clichés were so hilarious to me.

My dreams consisted of flash backs to different events in my life. Because of Thia drilling me about Yuri, as I drifted off into a deep sleep, I dreamed of her. She was a pretty little thing. Her long, black hair would flow effortlessly without so much as a nudge from a gentle breeze, eyes blacker than mine in my demon form, and a smile that would warm even the coldest hearts. She was a bit younger than my human years, maybe three or four. We met one day at school when some kids were teasing her and calling her racist names. Yeah, I always did have a thing for the weaker and more vulnerable ones. Despite being a vampire, it wasn't a habit of mine to want to sink my teeth into the first neck I came upon.

She seemed different than all of the other girls at school. Besides her obvious appearance, she was different in a lot of other ways too. She was quiet, meek, and very polite. She greeted everyone she met with a shy hello and a bow, something that was obviously reared into her from an infant. The other kids liked to make fun of her, mocking her name, the way she looked, and even referred to her as a Chinese slur; even though she was not Chinese at all. We bumped into one another as I was heading to my next class. Some students had rammed into her, causing her to lose control of her books and sent each and every one of them sliding across the hallway floor. She said nothing as she bent down to pick them up as the kids laughed and began to kick the books away from her as she would reach for them. She was humiliated and on the verge of tears when I approached her. The other kids, already thinking I was some sort of freak, slowly backed away in silence as I bent down to help her retrieve her books. She looked up at me shyly and thanked me for my help. After that day, we hung out regularly and I introduced her to Lee, Heratio, and a few of the other friends that I had. The only people I allowed to ever know my true identity and who I trusted above all.

Then we began to date. It wasn't anything steamy or hot. We just hung out and talked. She always had a lot to say even though she was typically quiet. I enjoyed listening to her.

It all came to a tragic end one day when she was in the car with her mother and a large truck t-boned them at an intersection. Her mother was killed instantly and she was severely injured. When news got to me I wasted no time rushing to the hospital where she had been admitted with multiple life threatening injuries. I was at her side and holding her hand when she took her last breath. She never regained consciousness. A part of me died with her that day. She felt like the closet thing I would ever know as a soul mate. She was my everything and I loved her deeply even though I never mustered the courage to tell her so when she was still alive.

As she lay before me, forever in a deep sleep, tears I never knew I possessed began to pour from my eyes. I laid my head on her chest and sobbed with such sorrow that I felt I would never be happy again. And it was only then that I had the courage to tell her how I really felt for her.

"I love you Yuri." I would say my final words to her as the bed side monitors all alarmed of her passing.

I woke from my terrible nightmare, reliving Yuri's life and death all over in my mind, with Thia shaking me.

"Lafayette! Are you okay?"

I opened my eyes wide and looked at her in a panic-stricken way.

"Yes. I was sleeping. What are you doing??"

"You were crying in your sleep. And mumbling something like 'Please, don't leave me!' and I was worried about you. Who were you dreaming about?"

I felt a little embarrassed that Thia had witnessed my dream from the real world and saw me crying. Was I really crying? I reached up to touch my face and felt warm moist droplets of tears.

"Yes. I'm fine. Just a bad dream; go back to sleep. Lee hasn't called yet so maybe by morning we will have some news."

Thia remained by my side as I lay back down to sleep. I

looked up at her as she starred back at me.

"What?"

"Lafayette... um... could I lie next to you?" She sounded nervous.

I lifted the blanket for her to get under. I turned, facing the opposite direction. She snuggled up next to me and wrapped her arm around me, putting her hand on my chest. I felt awkward, but I enjoyed having her close to me. At least for tonight, maybe my nightmares would ease up a little.

"I am really glad that we're together. I mean, the order paired us and I'm glad that it was you. I think you're pretty cool. Still a dumbass, but I think you will do just nicely." Her sarcasm had become more playful than at the start of our mission and it was everything in my will power not to turn over and show her just how much I enjoyed having her by my side. She would probably just punch me in the face or something like that to remind me what a bitch she was. As I lay there, feeling a bit turned on from having her warm body so close to mine, I was also becoming quite hungry and longed for the blood of something more satisfying than nearly raw beef. It seems as though I would have to wait for fresh blood just a bit longer and that in itself was frustrating as hell.

Early the next morning, my phone started ringing, waking me from a dead sleep. I reached over to the night stand to retrieve it and saw that it was Lee finally calling me back. The clock on my phone read 6:28 which for me was a bit early to get up. But alas, our mission was calling us. Or at least my new recruit for the mission was calling me. As I struggled to regain focus in my eyes from the blinding back light of my phone, I pressed the talk button.

"Hello?" I tried to sit up to get out of bed. I noticed Thia's arm and leg wrapped around me. I gently slid her body off mine so that I could move.

"Hey, Lafayette. I contacted the crew and they said whatever you need help with, they're game. So are you going to send us money to fly to England?"

I rubbed my eyes and yawned deeply.

"Yeah. Let me get woken up and get Thia up and ready and I'll head out to get you guys the money."

"Do I even need to ask how you are able to get thousands of dollars at the drop of a hat?"

"No, not really. Unless you want to live to see England, you might want to just leave that one alone."

"Yeah, yeah. I gotcha. Okay, I'll text you my info so you can wire that dough. We are all packed and ready to go so whenever we get the money we will catch the next flight out to London."

"All right man. Let me know just before you board and what airport you will be arriving at. Try to make it a night arrival. Those airport windows are hell on me, you know, vampire and all."

"Yeah, okay how are you able to walk in the sun? You *are* a vampire. Like the day you kicked ass and saved my miserable life."

"It wasn't sunny that day, remember? And the sun doesn't turn me into ash, man. It just burns like crazy and shows what I really am. Just get here okay? I need you guys bad. This mission is very important. Mankind's survival depends on it."

"Ah let mankind be damned. I am ready to leave this shit planet anyway."

"Lee!"

"Okay, man. Sheesh, so sensitive. You need to get laid, for real man. I can feel the pent up frustration from here!"

"When you get here, I am kicking your ass. Mark that in your to do list, 'get ass kicked by Lafayette.' Okay?"

"Will do. Text me an address where to meet you when we get in."

As I hung up, I shook my head in disbelief. Lee was as sarcastic and crazy as they came. I felt he could even give Thia a run for her money. I was grateful to have such a friend that I could call on in a moment's notice and he would be there for me no matter what.

Minutes later, Lee sent me a text with all of his personal information. I responded with the address of the place we were staying so he could find us. I turned to Thia who was still sleeping soundly and looking rather peaceful, and I gently nudged her with my elbow. She grunted a little but didn't fully wake. I thought of the pillow incident and decided against it. I didn't want to go there again, as it might get more heated after our kiss the night before.

"Thia, wake up babe. We have to get going."

Although she appeared to be in a deep sleep, she seemed to have heard that and immediately her eyes opened wide.

"What did you call me?"

Not wanting to repeat that again and save myself some humiliation, I figured a change in words would be the best option.

"Lee called, we have to get started with the day."

She rubbed her eyes and smiled.

"That's not what I heard." She reached up and touched my face with her hand. I smiled slightly and stood up.

"Come on girl. We have to leave. Hopefully the sun will stay hidden around here." I said trying to divert her affectionate desires.

"Oh, I just want to lie here with you a little longer." She stretched her arms and legs outward.

"Once I send the money to Lee, he'll gather his friends and head this way. We have a lot to do. And we need to be careful. That creature is still out there looking for us."

"LaFaytte, do you ever envy humans?"

"Why would I envy them?"

"They don't have to worry about constantly running from evil, or all of the things we do. They can fall in love and not worry about bringing demons into this world. Life is just so much easier for them. It's really not fair." She had a look of despair on her face which made me pity her.

I sat beside her and took her hand in mine. "This is the will of the gods. This is what they created us to be. We are not humans. We are demons, we are creatures of the night. We don't get to enjoy life. We just exist because it's what the gods wanted. We don't get a choice."

"Well I'm tired of this. I've been around a very long time. I've watched so many humans fall in love, have children, work jobs, and grow old together. I want that. I'm sick of this immortal life. I want to be happy." She took a deep breath and exhaled slowly.

It was at that point I found myself wishing the same thing. How cruel the gods were for creating us to be something we were never happy being. What made the humans so much better than us, that they were given the choice to enjoy things like love and happiness and we couldn't?

"Maybe when this is done and over with, the gods will grant us the things that we want."

"And if that happens, will me and you..." She paused and looked down at her hand in mine.

"You want me to say it, don't you?"

She looked back at me. "What do you mean? Say what?"

"Don't play with me Thia. Tell me what you want to say, and I will say what it is you want to hear."

She looked very nervous all of a sudden. "Lafayette... I... God, I can't believe I'm even thinking these words right now."

I moved in close to her, stared into her eyes and grinned.

"Thia..." I said slow and soft as I continued to smile.

She swatted at my arm playfully trying to excuse herself from saying anything. I pressed my lips to her for a quick kiss. Then I backed up slowly, still staring into her eyes.

"Stop that." She spoke in almost a whisper.

"Well since you are too chicken shit to say it, because you aren't the badass bitch I thought you were —."

"Oh I am *the* bitch. Don't you forget it!"

"I love you." I blurted out the words without further hesitation. I had finally forced the words from my lips and was as shocked that I had said them as she was, which was apparent by the look on her face. She said nothing. She just continued to stare at me. Her eyes seemed to tear up somewhat as she grabbed on to me for a hug. I knew she wanted to say it. But the hug said more than words ever could. I held her in my arms and we said nothing.

We left the hotel and headed to the nearest money wiring place. The sun was hidden behind dark gloomy clouds, which worked to my advantage. As we strolled down the sidewalk, I felt as if we were being followed. I looked over my shoulder but saw no one or thing that really stood out to me. I felt a bit apprehensive and my pace quickened. Thia noticed, but said nothing.

We arrived at our destination. I quickly darted inside and fished in my pocket for my debit card. The card contained all of the money that the Order would deposit into my account every month. It is how we would survive while here.

"Hi. I need to wire some money." I told the clerk standing behind a thick pane of bullet proof glass.

I handed him a piece of paper with Lee's information on it and the amount I wanted to send. The clerk typed in the information on the computer and told me to swipe my debit card. I took my card and ran it through the card reader and waited.

"I'm sorry, sir. Your card was denied. Insufficient funds."

"What? Try it again." I slid my card once again. *Denied?* I turned to Thia with a puzzled look on my face.

"What's going on?" I whispered.

"Here, try this one." Thia took her own card from her pocket and slid it.

"It's my own personal account. I take all the money from the card the Order gives me and transfer it to my personal account."

"God, you are a freaking genius. Which is why I love you so much."

She smiled sarcastically and then the clerk began to print off some paper work.

"Yeah, I know I am." She smiled back.

After the transaction was completed we walked outside and I texted Lee to let him know the money was on the way.

I turned to Thia. "So what made you decide to have the money they give you transferred to another account?"

"I guess you could say I'm not a trusting person and, though I never had any reason to think they would ever do this, I always assumed they could. Why do you think they withdrew all your money? They know you need it to survive here."

"I don't know. I think what Vick told us was the truth. They sent us here to die. They know we can't defeat the watchers! They are nothing more than pawns working for them and we got pulled into this so they could eliminate us. Dammit, how will we survive now?"

"Don't worry, I have plenty of money. I have been saving away for a very long time. It should last us for a while. But if they ever discover what I have done, you know they will do everything in their power to erase that account too."

"Well when Lee gets here, his friends can get our money back. They are computer nerds and can hack anything."

"I think it's best if we just leave it alone. Let's not stir up any more suspicion if we don't have to. And right now, they don't know that we're aware of their plan. We can live off my money."

I turned facing her. "You shouldn't have to. It's my job to take care of us."

She rolled her eyes. "Will you stop with that medieval bullshit? Women haven't needed to be taken care of in many years."

"You know what I mean." I glanced up at the sky which looked like it would drop buckets of water on us at any minute. I was starting to feel hungry. It seemed as though we would be eating nearly raw steak again.

As we found a place to dine on more human food, I couldn't help but still feel that someone was watching us. They weren't making their presence known, but I knew they were there.

We ordered our food and ate in silence. My mind was so heavy that I don't think I even looked at Thia the entire time we sat trying to scarf down the barely sustainable grub in front of us. I craved real blood. But I wasn't willing to kill to get it. I started to feel desperate enough to break into a blood bank and grab enough for a few days.

In my mind I went over our original mission. Find the watchers and take them out, to which they gave us no hint where they were or how they could be destroyed. I thought about what Vick had told us, that the Order had been infiltrated by the watchers. It's as if they had sent in a mole to gather information on beings like myself and Thia, sending us on a wild goose chase just to have us eliminated, thus preventing us from being able to stop the watchers.

We had been played in the worst way, but what exactly were the watchers planning? Why were we that big of a threat? Since we didn't even know how to take them out, why did they feel the need to eliminate us? I had so many questions and very few answers. For now, I would just have to wait on my friends to arrive and take it one step at a time.

As I ate, I felt a strange sensation in the pit of my stomach. At first I just believed it to be the nearly raw beef not agreeing with my demon digestive system. But then the hairs on my arm stood, a violent and very dark energy raced throughout my body and I could hear a faint whispering.

"Thia, do you hear that?" I carefully looked around, trying not to be obvious.

"Hear what?"

I said nothing else as I listened intently. Something wasn't right. This dark energy from the unknown started to burn me from the inside out. I gasped and pressed my hand to my chest. Thia quickly realized there was something not right at all as she reached over to take my hand in hers. I was gasping for air and could feel the burning becoming more intense.

"Thia, we have to go. Now!" I said in a low whisper. She slapped some money on the table and moved quickly to escort me out of the building. Outside, the sky was really black. As if a storm was approaching, but nothing about this felt normal. There was an evil here that I had never felt before and it was choking the life out of me.

As I continued my struggle to breathe, I leaned on Thia. She quickly led me from the building and away from the city. The clouds were rolling one over another, which gave them the illusion of an ocean tide being violently thrust against the shores from an oncoming storm. I was literally choking at this point and my vision became hazy. I felt like my life was slipping away from me. Everything was spinning. I heard Thia screaming my name in an absolute terrified tone. Everything went black.

CHAPTER FOUR
Creatures from the Abyss

As I began to awaken, I found myself lying on the ground with Thia kneeling beside me. She was shaking me and screaming my name. A sharp sensation pierced my skull with violent pain as I struggled to regain my senses. The sky was blacker than ever before and a strange howling sound could be heard approaching us quickly.

"Lafayette! Please get up! We have to hurry. I can't carry you!" Thia was sobbing. Her voice shrilled in a way that I'd never heard before.

I shook my head and struggled to my feet. Everything was still spinning and the urge to vomit was closing in on me as quickly as whatever dark force pursued us was. I had to pull myself together and find a place to hide. I looked up into the sky which had an eerie black thickness to it. I looked at Thia, who was obviously terrified.

"What is that?!" I yelled. The howling was getting closer and louder.

"Please! Let's hurry!" Tears were streaming down her cheeks and it was obvious that she knew something that I didn't know, and deep down it troubled me quite a bit. I felt vulnerable and exposed to whatever it was and I did not even know what "it" was or how to even escape it. I knew that Thia understood it and knew that we must retreat for our lives.

I grabbed her hand as we began to run. We did not know where we were or if we would even make it out of this alive. I did not even know where to go. I just knew we had to run. Thia struggled to keep up with me and kept glancing over her shoulder. It was so close now that I could almost feel it breathing down the back of my neck.

I spotted something off in a distance, a figure standing there amid the chaos, fearlessly challenging the dark force and signaling for us to run to it. As we drew closer, I recognized the old and bewildered face. It was Vick. We picked up our pace as did the thing chasing us. As we reached Vick, who stood holding a metal object in his hand, we collapsed beside him in exhaustion. In a flash, the howling ceased. There were no black clouds and the energy that I had felt only seconds before was gone. I realized that my eyes were closed. It seemed I had accepted my fate to this horrid beast. I slowly opened my eyes and we were not even in the same location. I scooped Thia up close to me as we both looked around at our new surroundings.

We were in a room with no windows and illuminated only by candle light. I was confused as I looked up to Vick, who was standing over us. He quickly shoved the metal object in his hand deep within his pocket and made his way to one of the blank walls. He touched its surface with his hand. I noticed a rippling effect in the wall. By now I was completely puzzled.

"What the hell was that?!

"A very dark and dangerous spirit."

"Yeah. I kind of felt that it was something evil. What's it doing here? What's with the clouds? How in the hell did we go from being outside to... wherever the hell this is?" I waved my arms around the room.

He turned and looked at both Thia and I with a look of dread on his face. "This is an illusion. I created it to conceal you from the darkness and to keep you here until it passes. While you are still technically outside where you were to start with, it cannot see or hear you. Call it an invisible barrier or such. For that darkness, you just vanished."

"Gods! I need something for this headache." I winced as I grabbed my head. It was still throbbing and the nausea had resettled into the pit of my stomach.

"Vick, I know exactly what that was, and why it was chasing us." Thia stood. She walked to the wall and slowly put her hand to it and closed her eyes.

71

"I expected you to know, since you have encountered it before, long ago."

I still had no idea what was going on or why I was feeling this way. Being sick wasn't exactly a vampire trait and I didn't like it one bit.

"Would someone like to tell me what is going on and what that thing is exactly, besides dark and dangerous spirit?"

Vick and Thia seemed to exchange concerned expressions that made me feel left out of a silent conversation.

"That thing out there, what is it? What does it want?" I persistently asked once again.

"It's a seeker. A creature tasked with locating and retrieving the key."

"What key?"

Vick cleared his throat and looked at me.

Vick reached into his pocket and pulled out the metal object I had seen him holding before. Something about it just resonated with me. I felt bound to it in some sense and pretty certain that I had encountered it before.

He held it up, its energy creating small particles of light that illuminated our surroundings with a soft white glow.

"This isn't just a pendant. It's part of a key. There are four pieces that when combined create the master key."

"A key to what?" Thia looked skeptical.

Vick slowly turned his gaze to her, "It is a key the gods gave four angels here on earth that were tasked with teaching mankind various things, helping them in a sense. Over the ages, as the angels began to mix with humans, the keys were lost."

"What do these keys unlock?" I was almost afraid of what he would say.

"In time, I will tell you everything. For now, just know that you have to protect this pendant from the forces of evil. And in return, it will protect you."

Thia seemed frustrated and anxious. As if she knew more than she was letting on.

I grew concerned about more of an immediate issue. "How will we know when that thing out there is gone?"

"This will let us know. It is a charm that detects evil and dark magic. As I stand here holding it in my hand, I feel the vibrations from it reacting to the darkness."

"I need one of those. Seriously, why wasn't I given one?"

Vick smiled but said nothing. Obviously this charm was only intended for certain people and not for a vampire who was the chosen one and destined to destroy that evil and save mankind.

"Lafayette," Vick began as he put the charm back into his pocket, "When we're able to leave this place, you and Thia need to go somewhere safe and stay there until you receive further instructions from me."'

"How will you get in touch with us?"

Vick's expression grew blank. He blinked at me a few times, reached into his pocket, and pulled out his cell phone.

"Well, okay, Yeah. Why didn't I think of that? A text message or a phone call. Sheesh, I'm starting to understand why Lee cracks so many jokes at me."

Vick was not a without surprise, that's for sure. He had the ability to create fake rooms out of nowhere and the old fella carried a cell phone. I giggled inside when I wondered what his ring tone might be.

Thia looked more nervous than usual, which made me a little more apprehensive. Though neither of them had fully explained my blood line link to this demon outside, I was sure that Thia would explain it to me later. My stomach grumbled. I knew I needed something sustainable soon. The beef was just simply not working for me at all. I felt malnourished and emaciated.

I had begun to hate this city. Not because it was always cold and wet, but because there was this lingering sense of doom and death in the air. I needed more answers than I was getting at this point. Something about Thia and Vick's interaction made me feel very uneasy. I had poured out my heart and, well, if I had a soul I would have poured that out to Thia as well. She seemed to be harboring a lot of secrets that I was not real comfortable with. I felt as if she didn't trust me enough to tell me what she really knew.

Back at the hotel that night, I didn't say much to her at first. I lay on the bed watching some boring British TV while she lounged quietly in a nearby chair doing something on her cell phone. I flipped through the channels until something caught my eye.

It was some sort of political broadcast with many of the world's top leaders. One in particular stood out to me. Although I didn't catch his name, one thing I did catch was his eyes. They were void of any soul. I watched carefully the way he made gestures with his body, his lips how they seemed to quiver and perspire, and his eyes, I just could not get over the eyes.

"Thia, look at this." She looked up seemingly annoyed that I was even in the same room with her.

"What is it?" Her gaze locked on the guy on the screen. A look of shock came over her and she quickly moved to sit by me on the bed.

"I know him!"

"Who is he?"

"I can't recall his name, but I have seen him around the order. He's kind of important and goes back and forth to the head council giving him information on other political leaders all over the world."

"Yeah and judging by his eyes, he isn't human. I wonder how many of them are in political positions."

"From what I hear, there are a lot of them. The order put them there as spies. Some of them, if not most of them, can't be trusted. Many have died under suspicious circumstances, or at least that's what the media says. I think the order has them taken out when they either betray their masters or become a liability."

I sighed, feeling frustrated and a bit annoyed that most of our time here was either running from something or trying to figure out what to do next. I took my phone from my pocket and looked at the time. Lee and the others should be arriving soon but we couldn't leave this room until we heard from Vick. I was

Amanda Zarovsky

still hungry and really wanted to leave.

"Ah!" I groaned as I stretched. "I need some food. Real food. I don't think I have had a decent drop of blood since I came here."

"Mmm, being a vampire has got to suck." She gave me a playful nudge and a wink.

"What about living for hundreds of years? That has to get old." She smiled and looked away from me.

"When you live as long as I have, you see things that no one else in this human world ever sees. Empires rise to power, they fall. You see generation after generation trying to fix the problems of the previous ones, and only making it worse. You see lots of death and destruction. Most of the time, you just wish that you could die. Or anything to escape the horrors of this world; looking forward to Hell because, really, Hell doesn't compare to this place."

"I haven't been around as long as you. But I have been around long enough to understand that this world is pretty much doomed. I don't even know what we're fighting for. What are we trying to save here? Humanity? This planet? What?"

"In a dog eat dog world, we are trying to save ourselves. That's really all that we can do."

Thia rested her head on my shoulder and wrapped her arms around me. I moved my arm around her and held her close to me. I turned my attention back to the politicians and world leaders and noticed there were more who weren't human. They were everywhere. They were in control of every decision made on this planet. That alone was frightening.

That night, I tried to sleep. I tossed and turned for the most part. Thia seemed to be resting uneasily as well. She gripped the pillow forcefully in her arms, her eyes closed so tightly they creased in the corners. She looked as if she were in pain. She moaned slightly and her breathing began to accelerate. I moved close to her and wrapped my arms around her. I hoped that even in her dream she could feel me and whatever horrors that invaded her dreams would simply go away.

She began to relax some. I felt confident that she was at peace now, so I drifted off to sleep.

土

My dreams of late had not been happy ones. Tonight was no exception. Once again I saw the darkness that quickly surrounded us, the screams that filled the air, and this creature that came out of nowhere to launch an attack on us.

I saw myself standing in an open field, clouds reaching down from up high and dragging their finger-like form onto the ground below. As they touched the earth I felt the ground shaking; I heard it moaning.

Just like a finger dragging through sand, the earth separated and deep from within, blood began to puddle out. The clouds moved furiously in the sky and fear had a choke hold on me. I dropped to my knees gasping for air and trying to make eye contact with the darkness. I couldn't see. I went blind. I could still feel its evil gaze on me. Screams from somewhere deep within the earth became much louder until the noise had reached deafening levels.

I heard the pleas of those already dead to save them from Hell. I knew there was nothing I could do for them. They cried out in a chorus of a million tormented souls and all I could do was cover my ears in a weak attempt to silence them. The grief of their suffering became too great and I buried my face in my hands to weep, but the moisture that fell from my eyes was not tears. I slowly lowered my hands to see them covered in blood. I wiped my eyes again, but the blood continued to pour out. I heard a raspy voice call my name. Slowly, I looked up to see a shadowy figure lingering above me. The blood clouded my vision and I couldn't make out the shape of it, but I felt it's hatred for me and it's will to destroy me.

The entire world felt like it was spinning out of control. I attempted to regain my footing, but was immediately hurled back to the ground by some unseen force. As I lay there helpless and afraid, I could feel this creature's hand pressing down on my back with such force I gasped for air. I turned my head slightly to the left and grimaced in pain.

A flash of light caught my eyes. It was coming from a small quartz crystal in the shape of a triangle with a rounded bottom. Light rays beamed from it in all directions. The moment this appeared I found myself inside of Vick's box.

I woke suddenly thinking about the object I had seen in my dream. I realized it was what Vick used to conceal us from that demon. I didn't know what it was exactly or what power it possessed, but I began to wonder if this was the pendant that the prefect spoke of.

I really began questioning things now. If that was indeed the pendant the order was seeking, what were their plans with it? Why did they want it so bad? And why did I feel so drawn to it? I felt as if I needed to drill Vick some more about the pendant, my mother, and my destiny. There was just something he wasn't telling me and that really bugged me.

I didn't go back to sleep after that nightmare. I felt uneasy and vulnerable, which kept me from getting any decent rest. I was also hungry. The Order be damned, I would need to feed soon. I was getting weaker and a weak vampire is a dead one.

Around 7 a.m. there was a knock at the door. I quietly and carefully made my way to the door, where I pressed my ear to it to listen. Then I heard a familiar and reassuring voice.

"It's just me, Lafayette."

I sighed in relief and began to unlock the door. As I opened it, Vick greeted me with two paper sacks and a smile.

"Room service."

I rubbed my aching head and stepped aside to allow him to enter. As he did, I quickly shut the door behind him. As I turned facing him, I continued to massage my temples where the pain was most intense.

"Here Lafayette, I think this will ease some of your suffering." He handed me one of the paper sacks. He glanced at Thia, who was still asleep. He turned facing me, a puzzled expression on his face. I quickly opened the bag to reveal its contents.

"Lafayette, you and Thia... you didn't —."

"What? No! Oh Gods, no! Sheesh. Who has time for all that

nonsense when we have demons after us all the time?"

I reached into the sack and pulled out what looked like a juice box.

"Apple juice?" I held the box up and examined it.

"Taste it. I promise you, it will make you feel better."

I was a bit reluctant. But his reassuring grin convinced me that it was okay. So I put the straw to my lips and gave it a slow suck. A very strong iron-like taste ran almost passionately across my tongue. I closed my eyes and moaned at the delicious taste.

"I told you it would make you feel better." He grinned.

"Oh! Indeed! But where did you get this?"

"Let's just say I have a few friends in high places that owed me a favor. Don't drink that too quickly. That is virgin blood, meaning blood that is pure and never tainted."

"This is excellent!"

I almost cried at the overwhelming sense of fulfillment I now felt. I took another huge gulp of it and savored the lovely taste.

"Like I said, drink slowly. Virgin blood will react to your weak system like vodka to someone who has never consumed alcohol."

Vick walked over to the bed where Thia slept soundly, oblivious to anything going on in the room. He reached in the remaining bag and pulled something out. It smelled sweet and warm, something I knew Thia would like. Almost immediately her nostrils flared. He placed it, fully wrapped in paper, next to her face. She opened her eyes wide, looked at Vick then at the delicious smelling thing in front of her. She quickly sat up and took it in her hands, sniffing it and sighing deeply with delight.

"Good morning Thia. I know your love for sweet things so I brought you this for breakfast."

She rubbed her eyes then quickly ripped into the packaging to discover a danish with thick white icing.

"Mmm, Vick! How did you know?" She smiled as she took a huge bite from it. I grew rather nauseous just thinking of the sweet taste. Those things never set well with me at all. There was far too much sugar in them. I wasn't prone to illnesses easily, I was certain a diabetic vampire would probably be the worst of them all.

"So Vick, how'd you know where to find us? I gave you my cell number. Not my hotel room."

Vick turned to me, "The wonders of modern technology. Anyone can be tracked these days with these blasted devices. Your location services are enabled. You might want to turn that thing off. Your social media site told me where you had checked in at."

Thia snickered as she devoured her breakfast.

I shrugged, not really caring at this point how he found us. The blood made me feel like a new man! I felt my strength returning and my headache almost instantly went away. The intense growling in my stomach was finally silent. Thia seemed equally satisfied.

My phone began to ring. Glancing at the screen, I saw it was Lee. I snatched it from the table and answered, "Yeah, hey Lee. Y'all make it in safely?"

"We're here, in baggage claim now. Man, this place is so dank, I feel like I am in a cave."

"Yeah. It always feels like that here. So do you want us to meet you somewhere?" As soon as I even hinted leaving, Vick quickly fixed his attention on me and raised a brow in protest.

"If you don't mind, we have no idea where we are and... there's this guy that is seriously freaking me out."

"What guy?" I was more than a bit worried now. When I said that, Thia and Vick shifted all attention to me.

"I'm not sure."

I could tell that Lee had the phone close to his mouth and spoke in a quieter tone.

"He was on the plane with us, kept staring at us, and now it seems everywhere we go. He's lingering nearby. I don't know man. I just have an eerie feeling about him."

At this point, so did I and I wondered if it was someone from the Order who had somehow overheard our phone conversation and knew he was coming here to help destroy the watchers.

"Hang on one sec, Lee."

I turned my attention to Thia and Vick. "Someone's following them. I think it may be someone from the order. We need to go meet them and make sure nothing happens to them."

"If you go out there again, you're risking your own life. We don't know exactly what is going on and until we do, you need to stay hidden," Vick insisted.

"I didn't bring my friends all the way here to abandon them when they're in danger. I'm going. You can come, you can stay... I don't really care, but I have to make sure that they're okay. And maybe find out who is following them. Thia, are you going?"

My question to her seemed to have caught her off guard. She licked icing from her finger tips and smiled.

"I would strongly advise against it, Thia," Vick warned.

Thia rolled her eyes mockingly at him. "Of course! I never miss an opportunity to be hunted down and most likely killed. Let's go!"

I rolled my eyes. "Your enthusiasm is more frightening than anything we could encounter out there."

"Lafayette, before you go, I want you to take this with you."

I held out my hand and he pressed something cool onto my palm. I looked to see it was the pendant that he had used earlier to conceal us with.

"This will protect you, but be careful with it. Its powers are very strong. Don't be careless with it and protect it with your life."

I looked down at it, finally able to really see its form. I saw an off-white triangle quartz rock. It was engraved with something that looked like a drunk had started a game of hang man. A thick line ran horizontal along the bottom of the pendant, almost to the edge. It wasn't perfectly straight, it was kind of wavy. A similar wavy vertical line was placed in the center of the bottom line. This marking didn't go through the other line, only up. Another horizontal line ran midway through this line, almost like a 't' but wavy like the others.

I looked up at Vick. The question I had in my head must have been obvious in my expression.

Vick nodded at the pendant. "The circle represents life, a full complete circle. The quartz represents the earth's energy. You will notice from time to time how it resonates. Pay attention to that, it could save your life. The markings are the language of the gods. Each pendant has its own engravings representing the four elements: fire, air, water, and earth. The one you possess is the element of earth. These are the things mankind fights over."

"Such a silly thing to fight over. The gods gave it to them so freely."

I put the pendant in my pocket.

"Indeed. And with those four things the watchers hope to destroy mankind, and are on a fast pace in doing so."

"Then I guess we had better hit them first and hit them hard, hmm?"

Vick sighed and looked at his watch. "Hurry and get your friends. Let's all meet back here and come up with a plan of attack."

"Thia? If you're done stuffing your face, can we go?" I turned to face her. She was still sitting on the bed, but had finished the danish. She was now licking the last of the icing from her fingers.

"Mmm. Yeah, I'm done. Let's go round up our posse and kick some ass!" She sprung from the bed way more cheerful than I had ever seen her be. Perhaps it was a sugar rush from that diabetes inducing pastry.

The train ride to the airport seemed to take longer than I thought it should. Maybe it was my anxiety from having to be out when I knew that creature was searching for me. Maybe it was seeing friends I hadn't seen in years. I wasn't sure what it was, but I just wanted to get there and back to our hotel.

As I sat silently scanning the faces of everyone sitting near us, I wondered if they knew what was really going on. Each one of them seemed to have only one purpose at the moment and that was to get somewhere. Most likely to jobs that made their masters rich while they struggled just to put food on the table. It seemed like a pitiful life to live and one I didn't envy. I felt sorry for them for being so naive and gullible.

Thia stared out of the window, seemingly in deep thought. I wondered what she was thinking and if she felt pity for the humans as well. Or maybe she was thinking about her long lost love. Whatever it was, she didn't want to share it with me.

I glanced over my shoulder and noticed a seemingly normal man sitting a couple of seats behind us. The hairs on the back of my neck stood on end alerting me that something was wrong.

I leaned in to Thia and whispered, "This guy behind us, something's up with him. I can feel it."

She turned her head from the window and leaned towards me for a kiss so that she could catch a glimpse of the thing behind us.

"He's not human." She moved closer to me.

"Yeah, I felt that. He's a dark one, I can tell."

"Let's get off at the next stop," she whispered as she kissed my ear lobe. This caused my entire body to tingle in a way that I didn't want to feel at the moment.

"Thia!"

"Just go with it. I'm watching him."

She moved her kiss down my neck. I closed my eyes and shivered. I was certain I let out a soft moan and then quickly cleared my throat. What a great time for Thia to put on a show in the presence of something that may want to kill us. For a second, I forgot about the thing behind us and enjoyed Thia's attention. I knew that she was doing it to curb suspicion, but I liked it nonetheless.

The train began to slow and we both quickly rose to our feet and headed for the door. She grabbed me and moved in once again for a kiss, all the while watching the figure to the back.

"He's beginning to stir. When we get out, we will have to make a run for it," she whispered.

As the train neared the stop, we both positioned ourselves for the run. The doors slid open and we darted out. The figure stood up, but did not pursue us. We hurried up a flight of stairs into the lobby area and stopped to look back. Seeing nothing, we were relieved.

"Why didn't he come after us?" Thia asked, somewhat out of breath.

I looked around, still not convinced that he hadn't.

"Let's go wait for the next train. Keep your eyes peeled. I do believe they're everywhere and soon we won't be able to out run them." We began to make our way back down to the train platform.

"I wonder if the others sent on this mission are being chased, too."

"I don't know. There are a lot of things I don't know. The order sent us to destroy creatures we don't know how to destroy. Vick gives me this strange pendant and the order had made mention of a pendant that they described looking like this. Where did Vick come from? How did he know we would be here? How did he know our names?"

"They sure are being secretive that's for sure."

We arrived at the platform and began to study the faces and movements of everyone that walked by. We had become quite paranoid on this mission and began to not trust anyone that approached us.

"When is the next train?" Thia asked.

I looked at the sign that hung from a brick column and waited for the info for our next train. "A minute and twenty seconds is what it says."

"I hope it's sooner." Thia's voice cracked as she looked around us. I pulled her close to comfort her.

"Just stay close. Try not to draw too much attention. Be aware of everyone that passes." I kept my head down close to her as my eyes scanned every person near us. I could feel her trembling in my arms as I tried to hide my own fear.

Finally the next train arrived and we quickly boarded and took a seat closest to the doors. This time the train was empty. No one else boarded with us, which was a relief. We could relax for a short while, at least until the next stop.

Strangely enough, at the next stop no one boarded the train on our end again. Once again we breathed a sigh of relief. Just one more stop until the airport.

As the train sped up I began to feel less anxious. As we neared the final stop at the airport, that fear hit me again. I didn't see anything out of the ordinary, but I could *feel* it.

As the train rolled to a stop, we both stood ready to exit as quickly and as less conspicuous as we could. The doors opened and as we stepped on to the platform we came face to face with the one who had been sitting behind us. His eyes were as black as the night, his skin gray like a corpse, and his breathing was hard and labored. We froze in an instant.

"Lafayette," it drawled in a low, raspy growl.

I could really feel my skin crawl. Thia locked her arms onto mine when the thing spoke.

"Who are you? What do you want?" I somehow managed to keep the fear out of my voice as I spoke.

He smiled at me and reached out with an old crippled looking hand. The ends of his fingertips ended in sharp, claw-like finger nails. I wasn't sure if I should make a run for it or stand and fight him. Both ideas seemed useless. He drug a finger nail across my chest and continued to smile. That's when I decided that I would have to make my next move. I quickly slapped his hand away from me and he let out a loud hissing cry. In the second that his hand was no longer on me, I grabbed Thia's arm and we began to run. This creature began his pursuit and turned out to be much faster than we were. In an instant it had caught up to us. I felt myself launched backwards by such force that when I hit the ground I rolled several times before coming to a stop.

I sprung to my feet with my hands up in front of me, ready to fight. I did not see the creature, or Thia. I began to panic. I ran to where I had left her, yelling her name. As I searched the area where she had last been standing, I put my hands on the top of my head and breathed heavy as I panicked.

"Thia! Where are you?!"

Others passed by me giving me pitiful looks as if they had not seen me being violently thrown to the ground, Thia, or that creature. My heart was racing as I frantically scanned the area for her, but to no avail. I took out my cell phone and dialed Vick's number.

"Vick! Thia's gone?!" I couldn't hide the panic in my voice.

"What do you mean she's gone?" His fear showed through in his tone.

"We were attacked by something. I was thrown across the platform and when I got up, the creature and Thia was gone!" I put my hand on my forehead and breathed heavily as I felt my eyes well up with tears. At that point I knew that I had made a huge mistake leaving the hotel. But the regrets would not help us now. I had to figure out where she was and get her back.

"Listen, Lafayette. How far are you from the airport?" Vick asked.

"We just arrived. We stepped off the train and this beast met us at the door!" I was literally screaming now and my voice cracked.

"Hurry and get your friends. Wait inside of the airport. I will come to you. Why didn't you use the pendant?"

I thought for a second. *Why didn't I use it?*

"We had no time. This thing came out of nowhere and caught us off guard. Oh my God! We have to find her!"

"We will. Just go. Stay inside until I get there. We will sort this out."

He was trying to be reassuring but I was in a full blown panic and nothing could calm me down. I did not want to leave the train platform, fearing that she might return. But I didn't want to wait for that creature to come for me too.

I remembered Thia had her cell phone and frantically began to dial her number. I became increasingly fearful when it went straight to voice mail.

"Oh God, Thia! What have I done?" I sobbed as I continued to look for her as I made my way to the top of the stairs. She was nowhere to be found.

CHAPTER FIVE
The Search for Thia

As I quickly made my way to the terminal where my friends waited, I still could not help but look around for Thia. I was concerned, but also heart broken. How could I allow something like this to happen? I should have been more prepared and more cautious. Vick warned us, but once again my pride got in the way of my better judgment.

I arrived to find Lee sitting patiently in a cozy looking chair and surrounded by several others that I did not immediately recognize. As I approached them, their expressions changed drastically from a warm greeting to realizing something was wrong.

"Lafayette, what happened man? You look like you have just seen a ghost." Lee stared at me wide-eyed.

"Thia, something took her."

"Wait, what? Thia, your girlfriend? Sidekick?"

"The girl I told you about. She was sent here with me and this creature has been stalking us. Before I could do anything, she was gone!"

Lee gave a concerned nod and turned to his friends.

"Well boys, it looks like the fun starts now. Lafayette, you remember Heratio?" A red headed guy stepped forward and extended his hand. Reluctant to touch anyone at this point, I just stood for a moment before receiving his handshake.

"Lee, we have to go. We have to find her!" I insisted.

"Lafayette, get a hold of yourself man. First thing's first, where was she taken?"

"At the train platform, just as we exited the train that beast appeared."

"What beast?"

A tall slender man with jet black hair cut in heavy layers just to his shoulders stepped up beside Lee. He wore glasses and dressed in urban street clothing. He resembled me in a sense, though I thought I was better looking.

"This is Asa, one of the best computer hackers on the planet. Trust me when I say that there is no system he can't get into."

"That's great and a pleasure to meet you guys, but we have to find Thia. Oh God! I need to call Vick!" I fumbled to retrieve my phone from my pocket.

"Who is Vick?" Lee inquired.

"He kind of just became part of the team. He said that he would meet us here." I dialed Vick's number, but it too went to voice mail. Frustrated, I shoved my phone back into my pocket and grabbed my head again with fear and anxiety.

"Damn Lafayette, I have never seen you like this bro. Are you okay?" Lee asked as he put his hand on my shoulder. I turned to him, my eyes red and swollen with grief.

"I have to find her, Lee. I love her. I can't lose someone else I love." I didn't want to break in front of the new people. They knew me as "The nice vampire." But I did not want to show any weaknesses to them just yet.

"Boy, you vampires, when you fall in love, it consumes you don't it? Hey, it's okay man. We will find her. I promise you that. So what do we do now?"

"Vick said to wait for him here. He will meet us." As I tried to explain the plan, I couldn't help but look around for Thia. My worst fears began to play up on me and I fought the demon inside of me that was aching to get out. I was much stronger than this. *Why had I allowed that creature to take her? I used to eat dark creatures like him for breakfast. Why was I not able to act faster with this one?*

"Come on man. Let's go sit and wait for Vick, okay?" Lee gave me a gentle tug. I looked at him and said nothing as I followed him and the others to an area with less people occupying it.

"Okay, so Heratio, Asa, this is my oldest friend. He saved my life more times than I can count and I owe him. Lafayette, if I die bite me, literally, so I can become a vampire too." For a second, his humor was exactly what I needed to calm down just a bit and I smirked slightly.

"You know it doesn't work like that," I went on to correct him, for a moment taking my focus off of Thia to resolve an ancient myth about vampires.

"What do you mean it doesn't work like that?" Asa asked.

"Well," I began, "vampires are not a product of being bitten by another vampire. We are born of the nephilim and a human. My mother was human. My dad, according to her, was an asshole. But a nephilim nonetheless."

"Ah. So if you bite me, what will happen?" Asa asked. I was really annoyed with the line of questioning, but understood their curiosity. It wasn't every day that mortals encountered creatures like us and engaged in civil conversation.

"Well it would hurt like hell then you would bleed. And at that point I could either drain the blood from you or take just what I needed and let you go. But of course, I could kill you if I wanted."

Asa immediately began to regret his question and sat back in his chair saying nothing else.

"But honestly, it isn't often that I would feed from humans so don't worry about that." I could hear their heavy sighs and they each turned to give the other a look of relief.

"Guys, I trust this man completely. So, trust me in saying he's one of the good guys. What you need to worry about are those other things; that which we are here to help put an end to." Lee said reassuringly.

Just then, I saw Vick approaching us from about thirty feet away. I was amazed at how quickly he arrived here.

I stood up to greet him as he drew closer. But as he neared us, I noticed a bewildered look on his face. He stood in front of me and quickly grabbed me by the arm, pulling me away from everyone and excusing us for a moment.

"That thing that took Thia, it was a creature from the Abyss." He wasted no time telling me.

"Well it sure as hell wasn't from London. The accent was all wrong." I joked but feeling somewhat defeated in my effort to lighten the mood any at all.

"It spoke to you?" He asked suddenly and fearfully.

"Yeah. It said my name."

Vick lowered his gaze to the floor and sighed deeply.

"What? What does that mean?"

"These creatures retain power over their victims by calling them by name. This renders the victim powerless. If evil knows your name, evil can destroy you just by saying it. You are lucky to be alive."

"If it wanted me, it would have taken me. It took Thia instead. What does it want with her?"

Vick looked back at my friends, then looked at me and made his way over to them.

"I apologize for my rude behavior. I am Vick."

"I am Lee, a friend of Lafayette's for many years now." Lee extended a hand shake.

"Pleasure." Vick spoke softly but with authority in his voice.

"This is Heratio and Asa. They are friends of mine with incredible skills."

"We will get into that later. First thing's first, we need to find Thia and we need to find her fast. We don't have much time." Vick looked at me and frowned.

I felt my stomach twist into knots and a lump rose up in my throat that no amount of swallowing would disperse.

"Sir, I have a question." Horatio raised his hand slightly.

"Yes?" Vick's gaze fell on him.

"There was this person following us. He was on the plane with us. Was he one of them?"

"I don't know, but it's very likely. The Order seems to be compromised and there is no telling what they sent with you guys. If indeed that was one of them, we aren't safe at all. They know you are here to help and they know that we have figured them out. We are all in danger now."

Vick's words were not reassuring to the others and I could tell they were regretting coming here. Except Lee. He seemed excited to actually be taking on something bigger than his boring miserable life.

"Lafayette, can you show me the last location Thia was at?" Vick turned to me.

"Yeah. It's at the train platform."

"Let's go then!" Lee added a bit in a hurry and more anxious than I was to return to that dreadful place.

As we made our way to the platform Thia disappeared from, I was instantly consumed with dread and apprehension.

I walked to the last place I knew Thia stood. I could still smell her scent as we approached. I could also smell the foul evilness of the creature that abducted her.

"We were running and right about here I was violently thrown back. I rolled a couple of times and when I managed to regain my footing, both Thia and that monster was gone."

Vick looked around, sniffed the air, and then bent down near the spot where she last stood.

"Was this here before?" He asked pointing to a dark smudge on the pavement. I leaned in closer to get a better look at it.

"I don't recall seeing it before. It may have been here, but I wasn't paying it much attention."

"Do you have the pendant on you?" He moved his gaze up to me.

"Yeah it's in my pocket." I reached deep into my coat pocket and pulled out the pendant. As I handed it to Vick, I wondered what he needed it for and what it had to do with Thia or the smudge.

He dangled the pendant over the smudge and it began to vibrate. I could hear a low whistling noise that seemed to be coming from the smudge spot. The pendant began to shake vigorously and sway back and forth.

Vick placed the pendant directly onto the smudge and put his hand out in front of him. I saw a ripple, as I did that day in the fake room, and he pressed his hand into the ripple until part of his hand disappeared.

"Whoa! What the hell is that?!" Lee took a step back.

Vick retracted his hand and looked up at me.

"That's a portal."

"This is a portal location," Vick said with a heavy sigh.

"So let's jump in and find Thia!"

"Lafayette, this is a portal to a dimension in Hell." Vick slowly raised his gaze to me.

"What does that mean?" Lee asked.

Vick sighed and stood up.

"This means that the creature that took her is something that was banished to the underworld."

The others shifted their gazes to one another and I was equally puzzled.

"What are you saying now?" I proceeded to ask.

"Hell is supposed to be sealed. Nothing goes in, nothing comes out. Unlike the other portals that have allowed beings to go from place to place on Earth and sometimes into Heaven, the Hell dimension was to remain locked."

The others listened in silence as they mentally tried to piece this puzzle together.

"So what opened this dimension?" Lee asked as he focused his gaze on Vick.

Vick sighed and looked at me.

"You did."

His answer was so abrupt that it took me by surprise and I shook my head doubtfully to protest.

"Wait, I am opening these portals? How?"

"The pendants have always possessed great power. But until now, they weren't able to open Hell. Until one was placed in your hand."

"I don't understand what is so important about me."

Vick sharply looked at me. "Because you are the last in the bloodline of Enoch."

I thought for a moment about what he had said. There is no way I could be a descendant of Enoch. He was righteous, pure, and I was, well, a filthy vampire.

"Your mother gave you something very special, Lafayette. Though she was a nephilim, she also comes from the lineage of Enoch. This makes you extremely special, and very valuable to the gods."

I didn't know how to process all of this. My blood line was that of someone great and holy. And here I was, a descendant, inadvertently unlocking Hell.

"Wait, wait, wait. I can't deal with this right now. I can't accept what you are telling me."

I turned away from them all and put my hand to my head.

"Lafayette, in time, the answers will come. But for now, it has begun. And whether or not you caused this, you alone must stop it.

I swiftly turned back to face him. I stepped closer to Vick, so close that I could hear him breathing.

"Okay, I did this then. I caused all of this. Now, how do we get Thia back?"

Vick cleared his throat and took a step back from me. "We need to find out what the government knows and how they are planning to use this to their advantage. They know you have one of the pendants, they understand its power and are trying to get it. And they seem to be tracking our every foot step. The question now is, how?"

Asa who had stood quietly for the most part began to chuckle. Everyone leered at him suspiciously as he began to shake his head.

"Do you have something to add here Asa?" Lee gave him a stern look.

"You're trying to track down these watcher dudes. They're all over the place and moving in ways we can't. You aren't going to find them or your girlfriend that way. This is just a hunch of course, but if the watchers control the elites of this world, or the governments, there will be a paper trail. Right?"

By now I had caught on and instantly grew very excited.

"Or a digital trail!" I added.

"Bingo!" Asa winked and pointed to me.

"You will have to explain this one to me." Vick was seemingly confused.

"I think it's time to head to the hotel and get busy!" I smiled, feeling a bit more confident.

"Dude, I seriously love your play on words." Lee smirked. Realizing the way I worded that, I felt a bit embarrassed. "Y'all are some filthy people! You know it?!" I scolded.

We made our way back to mine and Thia's hotel room and the nausea hit me again. The last time I was at that room, she was stuffing her face with a danish and talking about kicking watcher ass. Now, we would be arriving without her and it upset me. I didn't want to show that kind of emotion to the rest of the guys. Being a vampire, I had an image to maintain. On the inside, I grieved for her and hoped and prayed to the gods that abandoned me, that she would be okay.

Asa took a seat on the bed and took from one of his bags a laptop.

"Is it okay to sit here?" he asked me.

"Yeah man sure whatever you need."

"Okay. Mister Vick, sir—," he began.

"Please just call me Vick."

"These watcher dudes are controlling the world leaders, commanding their every move. This is what Lee briefed me on as we flew over here. I don't know your exact mission, but I know that these are some pretty nasty guys. And even though they're some sort of spiritual entities, their involvement with humans will make this a pretty easy task, at least for me."

"Okay, do explain." Lee sounded frustrated.

"In this day and age, most everything is digital. Hardly nothing is backed up on paper anymore and this includes government databases and files. They are stored in a mega computer somewhere that is supposed to be highly secure. Supposed to be… I, for one, can hack into most of them with ease. They really do sometimes use the wrong OS making their systems more vulnerable to nosy assholes like me."

"I am not sure what we can possibly find in some computer system that will help us, but carry on." Vick shrugged.

"Okay, let me see here..." Asa's voice trailed off as he typed in a website and attempted to log in to its server. In his first attempt he was denied.

"And that always happens, but it helps me to connect to the site via a bunch of terms I don't even want to try to explain because I will get a migraine. Just trust me when I say I know what I am doing."

"You're the man." Lee chuckled.

"They're pretty secure. They have firewalls and it always seems that their back doors are locked and bolted shut. But, it's just a matter of time and something about binary coding and yadda yadda and..." He typed up a series of letters and numbers that made no sense to me and at once, he was in.

"Viola!" He looked up at Vick, who was staring at the screen in astonishment.

"Sheesh, and here I am struggling to figure out how to change the ringtone on my phone. Maybe you can do that for me Asa?" I joked.

"Of course," he laughed. "What would you want it to be?"

"Hmm... well there was this song that was famous in the 80's, something about Hell."

"Ah, of course, that is so fitting, you know, whole vampire-demon thing." Asa laughed.

Lee held up his fingers in the famous rocker devil's sign. "Rock on, dude!"

"Lee, you really need to update your style man." I couldn't help but laugh.

As we all stood around watching Asa pry into the most secretive documents on the planet, fascination was intertwined with apprehension. I knew that we may discover things we didn't want to; things that would force our hand at some sort of intervention. I just knew that right now, we had to figure out where Thia was and who was behind her abduction and if it had anything to do with the watchers and the world elites.

"Well this is interesting." Asa studied some script he had uncovered.

We all leaned in towards the computer to get a glimpse of

what he was talking about.

"There are a series of numbers one after another. Hang on." Asa opened a new tab on his browser and began to type in the numbers from the government web page.

"Are those what I think they are?" Heratio's eyes were wide with shock.

"If they are, then we may have stumbled onto something." Asa nodded.

"Okay, translate here, I don't speak nerd!" I demanded.

"These numbers, they are coordinates. Each one pin points a specific location. There are several dozen here. We need to start writing them down. Okay, the first one is in Washington, DC. I guess that is no shock, nor do we need to wonder why that is on the list. The second one here is in Australia. Another in Saudi Arabia and…" He paused, checked the next number, then pulled up another map and typed in the numbers. He clicked on an earth view of the location and zoomed in.

"What does that look like to you?" He looked up at me.

I looked, and my mouth dropped wide open.

"That's the train station! But what does that mean?"

"Well, it could mean that our good old trusted government put that location in their files because it's significant and it makes me wonder with all of the others, just what do these areas mean. If you'll notice, each of the areas listed here, and I have only managed to make out four of them so far, seem to be very important places; except your train station. I mean it's a freaking train station not the White House. So what is the connection?"

"What's the location of some of the others?" Lee leaned in closer to the computer screen.

"Well let's see…" He typed in more numbers and pulled up more locations.

"Israel, Afghanistan, Turkey, and… China? Well, okay that one didn't seem to fit the others, but it is what it is. What could be their reason for needing to save these locations?" He gave each person in the room a questioning look.

"Those are portal coordinates." Vick heaved a deep sigh.

"And how do you know this?" I asked, turning my attention

to Vick.

"Why else would they have a pointless train station in the mix, the same train station you and Thia were attacked and where she was abducted?"

It made sense really.

"So the government has a file in their computer database listing the exact locations of portals?" Heratio added. "Does it say anywhere in there if these are earthly portals or... whatever the other one was that Mister Vick here mentioned before?"

"No, I don't think so. It doesn't really list anything at all except the numbers. There is, however, a star beside a few of them. We need to jot that down and research those locations to see what makes them special enough to have a star."

"Okay, you guys start writing down those locations. Let's see if we can piece this together. Lee, what do you remember about our conversation many years ago, when I first told you about the fallen angels?"

"Well, I remember you saying that there were some good ones and there were some bad ones. Apart from that, I can't recall much of our conversation back then. I may have been drunk." He crinkled his nose and gave me a somewhat embarrassed look.

"I swear Lee, if you had been sober most of our teenage years, you could have learned so much from me." I shook my head in disbelief to his immature ways growing up, or lack of growing up.

"Maybe, but your whole vampire-watcher-demon crap is what drove me to start drinking. You're lucky I didn't need therapy after hanging out with you some nights."

"There are good watchers, yes," I continued, ignoring him. "Vick was a watcher, so was Thia. Then there are some really evil ones that have no place in Heaven, but cannot yet be cast into Hell. Those monsters are roaming freely on this earth, doing as they please, and in their evil plans they use human pawns —."

"To find the key!" Vick cut me off.

"The key that I now seem to possess a part of. Thank you very much Vick." I couldn't contain a sigh.

"It is possible that the creature believed Thia had the pendant." Vick spoke up in his defense.

"Well, okay, so I'm sure by now it knows that she doesn't have it. Now what?"

Vick shook his head, "That's one of the questions I honestly don't have an answer for. Asa, let's get all of those coordinates written down and let's start researching them more. You and your guys can do that since you are good with computers. Me and Lafayette will try to find out what this demon wants with Thia and hopefully locate her before it's too late."

I quickly looked at him with fear in my eyes. *Too late? What exactly did he mean by that?*

"Too late?" I stared into his eyes.

"I don't want to cast any doubt here, but if she was abducted by a demon from Hell, then she is in great danger and our options are even more slim now."

I had had enough of the back and forth and at this point I was not thinking clearly.

"So let's just go back to that portal, open it up, and I will go in and find her."

"You could be walking into your own death trap by doing that," Vick warned me.

"You obviously didn't consider that when you handed me this damned pendant, knowing what it could do, and failing to tell me about it."

The others in the room grew quiet as the small squabble broke out.

"I'm sorry Lafayette. I should have told you everything about it. But —."

"Just don't talk to me, unless you can give me a better idea then jumping into that portal."

"You may not know how to destroy them yet, but they know how to destroy you," Vick cautioned.

"Then if that is what is meant to be, so be it. We have to stop this once and for all. If my only purpose in existing was to die to save mankind, then that is what will happen."

"Hey guys… I think I found something else!" Asa was staring

intently at the computer screen. As we all shuffled to gather around the computer again, Vick seemed very uneasy, as if we were onto something that he didn't want us to know.

"What's this?" Lee asked.

"Well, it's another portal location. This one has a time by it, fifteen minutes from now exactly one mile from the train station. I wonder if this means that in fifteen minutes, a portal will open. I think we need to rush to this location and get a firsthand glimpse into what is coming in and out of this world."

"Let's go then!" I headed toward the door.

"Wait," Vick interrupted. ""If the watchers are aware that you can open these portals, then they would alert the government as well. You could be walking into a trap."

"Perhaps. But at this point, I don't think we have much of a choice. It's not like things are going to get better if we just sit around and wait. We have to just face these fears and dangers head on. And I for one am sick of running. I am sick of hiding from what I don't know and understand."

"We must use extreme caution. Something about this one doesn't feel right to me. Hang on to the pendant. And take heed of its warnings."

I looked at the others and just nodded my head. I was certain that we would face something dark and evil when we arrived. But nonetheless, this was our mission and there was no way I would back out now.

I didn't fully understand the pendants, but knowing their power meant we had to find and destroy them before they could be combined and used for whatever evil the watchers had intended.

I was worried about Thia. I hoped that wherever she was, she was okay, and knew that I was thinking of her.

CHAPTER SIX
Ruax

The sounds of grinding metal were excruciating, but worse were the desperate sounds of gnashing teeth and demonic snarling. In the darkness of oblivion, Thia hung from some sort of tree like object; completely bound and gagged. The sounds of suffering enveloped all of her senses, driving her to a moderate level of insanity. Tears began to trickle down her cheeks as she could only imagine what her prison looked like. She could smell death as if it were rubbing its rotten finger against her nostrils. The heat inside of this prison was so intense she found it difficult to breathe.

She felt the gag aggressively snatched from her mouth, causing her to gasp for air as if she hadn't breathed in a long time.

"Who are you? Show yourself!"

She heard a sinister chuckle followed by a hard kick to her stomach. She flinched, unable to completely shield her body from the blows, gasped for breath, and composed herself.

"So this is what you do? Tie people up and torture them? And for what?"

"You talk too much. I see now why the gods abandoned you." She heard a sharp voice hiss.

"And what about you? What's your story? You obviously aren't in Heaven now are you?"

She felt a sudden wave of anger and resentment emanate from her captor. It growled and threw something which caused a loud crashing sound. She felt a swift movement towards her, which caused her to draw up in anticipation of another kick. Instead, she felt a hand grab her around the throat and squeeze.

"If you weren't so important, I would kill you myself. You are starting to get on my nerves."

Under the tight squeeze of the creature's hand she managed to take a breath to speak.

"Well, the feelings are mutual."

The grip on her neck tightened. The blinder was painfully ripped off her head. She squinted her eyes, trying to regain her focus until she could see a shadowy figure standing before her. She blinked a few times before her eyes opened wide. It was not the same creature that had attacked them earlier.

"Ruax!" *Thia whispered in shock.*

"It's good to see that you remember your old friend." *He chuckled, returning to a make shift table with some metal objects on it.*

"We were never friends!"

"We could have been. We could have been a lot more, too. But you decided to play footsie with these disgusting humans."

"I did my job, unlike you."

He turned back to look at her, his long black hair waved across his shoulders by the motion of his head abruptly turning.

"Your job? You were banned from Heaven just like me and so many others. Your only job was to live and serve these wretched humans for all of their natural born lives. You never even tried to regain our position with the gods. You caved like the little bitch that you are. And now look at us."

He slowly stepped towards her until she could finally take in the details of his face. He was one of the most beautiful angels that the gods ever created. Even Lucifer often felt envious of this angel's splendor. Unlike most fallen angels, whose eyes were brown, his were a crystal blue. His complexion was as pale as porcelain and equally flawless. To any average human, he would be the definition of perfection and beauty. His eyes slanted upward with long lashes that curled at the tips. He dressed in all black, accented by a black robe. He could easily seduce any woman, and perhaps even any man that he so desired. But his hatred for the humans kept him at a fair distance from them.

"I did what I could. I tried to reason with them. They wouldn't listen."

"Ah Thia, you are so naive. It's a wonder that you even made it this far. You couldn't even see their plan right from the start. The gods orchestrated the entire rebellion."

"Why would they do that?"

Ruax sat down on a large rock near Thia and smiled.

"Let's just call it entertainment for the gods. They created those filthy humans to rile us up so that we would rebel. That gave them a reason to be assholes and kick us out. We never meant anything to them and now that they had the humans they didn't need our love or praise anymore."

"Well then let's do what is right and get back in their good graces."

"Oh Thia, so gullible. How it would arouse the egos of the gods if we did that. No. I for one want to destroy their lovers, these ghastly humans. When I have broken their heavenly hearts, I plan to destroy the gods too."

"Do you really think you are any match for the gods? They created you. They can destroy you."

"Of course they can. Except..." He stood and walked to a voided, black area along the wall. He stretched out his hand and instantly an image of a garden appeared.

"They are bound by morals and creeds. When they command something, it's set in stone and never changing. Once in a while they slip up and do something incredibly stupid."

He turned back to her and grinned.

"Do you see this beautiful place?" He motioned to the illusion before him. *"This was once mankind's perfect paradise. Everything they needed existed in this place. The gods created everything good, but in all their good they also created evil. It's the laws of the universe that in order for there to be good, there also has to be evil. To have darkness there first has to be light. The yin and the yang of the cosmos, because of this their system of power has a weakness. When they created this beautiful and perfect paradise, they gave man everything he would need to sustain his life, but he also planted an idea that ultimately lead to humanity's fate, death. The gods are clever and, seeing their mistake, they decided to restore what they had originally intended for the humans by also planting this beauty."*

Thia watched as the image before her zoomed in on a creepy looking willow tree. It stood between two stone pillars with huge fire balls on each side of it.

"Yes, that is the gods' mistake. The Tree of Life. They didn't want

101

their beloved humans to die for all of eternity. So they gave them a passage out, thus making a passage for us watchers and vampires as well."

"You're trying to get to the Tree of Life? No one can get to it. No one knows where it is." Thia insisted.

"Oh, but there is one who does. One that tried to educate these humans on the ways of the gods. One who was discarded like trash and made to spend millennia on Earth; locked away in some mountain, forgotten by the gods and their favorite ass kissing angels. It is Azazel. We will locate and release him so that he may have vengeance on mankind and the gods. He is the only one who has not only seen the tree of life, but has tasted its fruit as well."

Thia bore a look of panic. She began to hyperventilate. Ruax noticed and laughed loudly.

"Oh you didn't know? Your beloved Azazel was the one who led the rebellion. He was thrown out with you and you never knew!"

He continued to laugh hysterically and Thia found herself becoming engulfed by the rage in her heart. Ruax somehow knew of her love for Azazel and was using her emotions against her.

"So I guess now you have to ask yourself, where was your Azazel after all of those years that you cried for him and begged the gods to take you back just so that you could see him again. Now you find out that he has been here all along and not once did he try to find you. Oh, this is rich. If only you could see your face now."

Ruax continued to laugh in a demonic and unsettling way, taunting her with the grief from her own heart. Thia began to sob even harder now as the pain in her chest began to build up. She could no longer contain the agony in her chest and let out a blood-curdling scream that shook the walls that surrounded her.

I said nothing as we rode the train to the platform nearest the next portal. We only had a few minutes to spare and the closer we got, the more anxious I became. What exactly would emerge from this portal? Would Thia somehow find her way back through it?

The others sat quietly and somewhat distant to each other, as if they were in their own thoughts. I paid close attention to Asa. Though he was very intelligent and seemingly helpful, something about him just didn't sit right with me. I wanted to believe that Lee wouldn't bring anyone into my midst that couldn't be trusted. I looked at my watch. Three minutes to spare. I felt around in my pocket for the pendant that Vick had given me. I did not fully understand its purpose or even its powers, but it had saved me once before.

As the train came to a halt, something inside of me stirred. I followed the others off the train and we made our way to the suspected location. I felt the pendant inside of my pocket begin to vibrate. I stopped dead in my tracks, staring off into the distance as if I were being called there.

"Lafayette, come on. We only have a couple of minutes." Asa's voice sounded rushed.

I didn't move. I paid attention to the feeling inside of me telling me to follow the vibrations of the pendant. The sky began to darken and the wind whipped around us violently.

"Lafayette! It's coming!" Vick shouted, barely louder than the whistling of the wind. As the others stood frozen with fear, I gripped the pendant tighter in my hand. It was violently shaking now.

"Everyone, get back!" I could feel something inside of me reaching out towards the heavens. The rest of the group hurried to a safer distance as I began to take steps towards something I could not yet see. A bright flash lit up the sky and a loud boom penetrated the ground below me, knocking me onto my back. As I fell, the pendant dropped from my grip and landed on the ground a few feet beside me. I scrambled to retrieve it as a swirling light appeared before me. I was almost numb with fear as my hand finally grasped the chain of the pendant. I hurried to regain my footing.

I saw the others shielding their faces from the dust that was kicked up by the wind. I waited for what would come out of the swirling vortex of light.

A being emerged from the portal; he was tall with dark hair with fierce blue eyes. He radiated with such energy that it was blinding to me and I quickly covered my eyes to escape the glare. I heard a growl and a sinister laugh. I lowered my hand to catch a glimpse of this fearsome creature.

He appeared to be a man, a very handsome one at that. Though he was covered in light, I could feel darkness inside of him. He extended his arm towards me and I heard him call my name.

I squeezed the pendant in my hand and closed my eyes. I ran towards the creature full force and as we collided, everything went black. When I opened my eyes, I could not hear the wind or my friends. All I could see was pitch darkness except for the beast in front of me. He stood with a grin on his face. I looked around, but could see nothing else.

"Do you really think your tricks would work on me, Lafayette?"

I composed myself for whatever he may try next. Instead of attacking he just stood grinning, which was more unsettling than a physical attack. It was as if he was toying with my fear and apprehension.

"Who are you? What do you want?"

"Ah, what do I want? Hmm, now that is a loaded question." He followed with a deep raspy chuckle, "I want humanity exterminated. I want to reclaim my position with the gods. I want creatures like you who have betrayed your own kind to suffer for all of eternity in the deepest and most agonizing pit that Hell has to offer."

"Who did I betray? I am not like you."

"Oh but you are, Lafayette. The same blood that flows through my veins also flows through yours."

My eyes grew wide and my mouth dropped open.

"What?"

"Oh yes, let me introduce myself. I am Ruax, but you can call me Daddy."

For a moment, my mind raced back to what few memories I had as a child and what I remembered my father looking like.

He was indeed beautiful, which is how my mother was so easily seduced by him. And from my memories I knew that he was very manipulative and anything that he said at this point could not be trusted.

"You... you destroyed my mother. Did you know?" I clinched my teeth as I fought the anger that rose inside of me.

"She was nothing to me. Just someone to carry out my will. Unlike that beauty of a girlfriend of yours."

"Thia?"

"How pitiful it was to see her pine away after her old lover. She never really got over him you know."

The more he talked, the more I just wanted to punch him. What an arrogant bastard he was. I knew I would have to control my emotions if I wanted to live, and find out where Thia was.

"Where is she? Where is Thia?"

"She's here, somewhere. I don't think she wants to come back to you. See, I made a deal with her that if she gives me what I want, I would give her what she has wanted since the beginning of time; her lover who was cast out of Heaven and locked away deep inside of a mountain, his own personal hell if you will. I know where he is and I can get him out. Needless to say, your beloved Thia was more than eager to work out a deal with me."

I didn't know if he was telling the truth or saying all of that just to spite me. Surely Thia wouldn't betray me just to get back with a former lover. I had to trust that what we had together was real. At this point, I wasn't sure if I could even trust myself. I had allowed myself to break one of the cardinal rules and that is to never fall in love. I had become blinded by my own emotions and I realized how weak it had made me.

"And what do you want?" I was trying to completely ignore all that he said about Thia.

"Well, I want to break out our beloved Azazel, eradicate this plague called humanity, and regain the love of the gods as we once had."

"I suppose you already know how you'll do this."

"Of course. I didn't just barge into this filthy world without a plan." He glared at me and smiled. There was something charming and seductive about the way he smiled. I wondered if he had used that same expression on Thia to get her to succumb to his evil intent.

"You see, Lafayette, in your hand is an item that can not only enclose us into your own altered reality, but it has the power to do so much more. It once belonged to the angels, along with three more just like it. Somewhere along the lines of time that only exists in this world, the humans managed to get their hands on them and we have been trying since to reclaim them all."

"Oh, so you need something I have because you aren't powerful enough on your own?"

As the words left my lips, he charged towards me, almost as if he were floating and stood only centimeters from my face.

"Don't temp fate, Lafayette!" He snarled at me. "I could destroy your entire existence right now if I wanted to and I don't need help from some pendant." He slowly backed away from me and I heaved a sigh of relief.

"Then why are you here?" I asked as he took another step backwards and turned away from me.

"I want that pendant, but I cannot just take it. It is loyal to the one who possesses it and does not easily commit to another. You have to release its loyalty into the hands of a new owner."

"And what makes you so certain I would ever do that?" At that moment, I felt as if I had the upper hand. I had what he wanted and he could not physically take it from me. Somehow that was empowering.

"Well, if you don't, I will return to the other side where your precious Thia is and I will slowly rip her to pieces until nothing remains of her but the darkness in her heart, then I will come find you and do the same to you."

My heart raced with fear as I tried not to think about anything happening to Thia.

I thought long and hard about what he said and what I knew Thia would say to him if she were in my shoes. She would tell him to go to Hell and would never give up the pendant. It is something I would have done too, had I not fallen in love.

"Tough decision, eh? Give me the pendant, which you know

can save all of humanity, and rescue your princess. Or watch everyone that you love die. I know how hard that must be considering your pathetic immortal side is weakening to the desires of your human side."

I did not know what to do. I felt so conflicted inside that it was making me physically sick. I fought the burning in my eyes and the urge to just go for him. My anger and fear were starting to affect my rational thinking. *What would Vick do?* Vick would sacrifice himself to protect the pendant.

"Come on Lafayette. Just listen to your daddy. No one on this earth is worth dying for. If you would join us, you would see that. You could be so powerful. Why throw all that away for these maggots that have hated your kind since the beginning of time?"

"Because that is who we are, Ruax. Though immortal, we still possess the human characterizations of love and compassion, something you obviously know nothing about."

He grinned again and shook his head.

"Oh, I know love. A love like you have never known. The love from the gods that no human or creature on this planet can compete with. And the humans stole every bit of that from us. And then…" He paused and turned his cold dark gaze to mine. "Then there was your mother."

The second he mentioned my mother again, all of the rage and hatred I had for him began to burn inside my chest. All of the years that my mother referred to him as the "dead beat loser" just seemed amplified by his presence. I had never known him. Now I understood why my mother hated him so much.

"Your mother stole my heart. Like no human could. She was fair, beautiful, and oh so kind. So unlike any other human I had met. She said she loved me. I thought she did, until you were conceived and I was forced to reveal my true nature. Of course, she rejected the idea that I was immortal and even more so that she was a nephilim and would bear a vampire. This was too much for her to take and she told me to leave." He turned his back to me and I could hear him breathing hard and anxiously.

"My mother loved you. She said you abandoned us." There

was spite and hatred in my voice.

"Oh, Lafayette. Your mother is a good liar. She brainwashed you all of your life. She told you that you were not like the others. That you were a creature of the night. Did she bother to tell you where you really came from?" He turned back to me and his eyes changed in color from a crystal blue to a black.

"Well, no." I thought for a moment and realized my mother had never been completely honest with me about my heritage. For a second, I began to resent her for it. Now, I was looking at the man that I had believed abandoned me for answers.

"Of course not. That is how she protected her dear son." He chuckled and slowly began to walk back towards me. Each step he took echoed in my head like thunder rolling. I could feel his power with each breath I took. He was clearly something more than my mother had allowed me to believe that he was. He wasn't *just* an angel.

"Your mother was one of the last descendants of Enoch. Her blood is so powerful that angels shudder in her presence. Even I, the first time I met her, knew there was something special about her. Unlike other nephilim, she was more human and compassionate. That is how she lured me into her web. The same blood that flows through her veins flows in yours. You, Lafayette, being the son of a daughter of Enoch, you are also the son of the most powerful being that ever existed in this world. That makes you very, very powerful."

As he moved closer to me, I could feel my heart pounding in my chest. A certain excitement was aroused in his presence and also a certain fear.

"I'm not powerful. I can run fast. I can slip away unnoticed in the dark, but I'm not powerful." I argued, clearly he knew something that I didn't.

"You don't even know your own self-worth, and that is sad Lafayette. Your two-faced bitch of a mother should have raised you to know who you are and to nurture those gifts that you possessed at birth. She should have realized your importance. But instead, she wanted to make you as human as she could to ease her own mind of the abomination that she carried and gave birth to. You can think that you are like them, but you are not. Your hunger can only be satisfied with human blood. The sunlight exposes the darkness inside of you. You cannot even consummate your love to Thia without fear that you will create something just like yourself. What exactly are you left with? You cannot even co-exist with these humans because the temptation is just too great. So why do you do it? Why not join me and we can rule this world together. We can rid this world of these parasites called humans."

I lowered my head, ashamed to admit that he was right. Why was I fighting so hard to save the ones that had always wanted to wipe out my kind? What were these humans worth? They are greedy, selfish, and turn on each other to fulfill their lust for more wealth and power. For a moment, I asked myself why I was trying so hard to save them. The answer was clear to me.

"I do it because it's the right thing to do. I don't have a soul, not like them. I don't have the love of the gods. I am lower than a worm that burrows through the dirt, but this is my destiny. This is why my mother and you created me. I am here to destroy you and save humanity."

With that, I sprung from my seated position and lunged towards him. Catching him off guard, I wrapped my hands around his neck. A storm surrounded us as the evil inside of him struggled to defeat me.

The howling of the wind as it rotated quickly around us became deafening. The pendant crawled its way out of my pocket and hovered beside me as if it were being called. He noticed it and slowly extended his hand as if to grab it.

"Join me, my son! Let's put an end to this war and suffering!"

I snarled and my grip on his neck tightened.

"Where is Thia!"

He laughed and then coughed as my grip began to choke him. "You will never see her again unless you give me that pendant."

I looked down at the pendant stretched out towards him and knew that if I gave it to him he would destroy the world with it. If I didn't give it to him he would destroy Thia, myself, and everyone I knew. Tears fell from my eyes and rolled down my cheeks as anger consumed me. If I really was what he said I was, I knew I couldn't let him win.

The power of the pendant was becoming too strong for me and my grip on his neck started to weaken. He must have sensed this and seized the opportunity to shove me backwards away from him. As I fell to the ground, the pendant slipped from my grip and slid across the ground towards him. As the swirling vortex of chaos continued, the pendant began to emit a light that was so bright I threw my arm up over my eyes to shield them from the intensity.

The pendant began to violently shake as Ruax's hand slowly reached for it. He knew that he could not take it from me unless I released its power to him. I knew that if I didn't, he would kill Thia. It was in that moment that I knew what I had to do.

"If you want the pendant, you will have to search for it!" I focused all of my will and quickly reached for the pendant, grasping it in my hands, and then facing the direction of a portal that had begun to spiral quickly as it opened.

I raised the hand that held the pendant and I heard Ruax scream, "No!"

I threw the pendant inside the portal. In a flash, I was back outside with the others and there was no sign of Ruax. I was lying face down on the ground, a bit disoriented as the others quickly filed around me.

"What on Earth happened?" Lee frantically asked as he reached for my hand to pull me to my feet. I looked up and around at everyone, who's wondering eyes were fixed on me.

Then I looked at Vick who appeared relieved that I was back and safe.

"He has Thia," I said as the tears began to fall down my cheeks.

"Who?" Vick asked approaching me.

"Ruax. He's the one that attacked us. He wanted the pendant. He said if I didn't give it to him, he would kill her."

Vick sighed. "Ruax is not to be trusted in anything that he says. He is manipulative and malevolent. So where is the pendant?"

I lowered my head to sob.

"Lafayette? Where is the pendant?" He seemed more concerned about the pendant than whether or not Thia was alive and this bothered me.

"I couldn't give it to him or withhold it from him. As a portal opened up near us, I threw the pendant in it."

"You did what?!" Vick shouted.

"I didn't know what to do, okay!" I cried out. "He was going to kill her. So I sent him searching for the pendant. In the mean time we can try to locate Thia and then go after the pendant. At least now he knows that I don't have it so that gets him off my back." I looked at the others who had a look of disappointment on their faces.

"What would you all have done? Huh? Do you think it's easy to make a decision like that? So don't give me those looks. Don't bitch at me. You weren't the one trapped in darkness with that beast! Who, just happens to be my father."

Vick's eyes grew wide and he stuttered, "What?"

I turned a glare towards him and wiped my tear-soaked face.

"Don't act like you didn't know. Don't you dare stand there and act like all of this comes as a shock to you." I stumbled to my feet and felt my weak body sway in my attempt to balance myself. I continued to stare at Vick.

Vick sighed as if defeated. "Yes, I knew. I am sorry that you had to find out this way. By now I hope you know how special you are though."

I couldn't even find the right words to say to him that didn't translate into him pleasuring himself with a baseball bat wrapped in barbed wire. I was furious and I felt betrayed.

"My asshole father is a freaking angel. And not just *any* angel, He is one of the originals! How much more are you going to keep from me? I am sick of this mission and sick of your deceit!"

"I am sorry, but we need to get that pendant."

I paused and just stared at him. "No. I need to get Thia back. Do you even care about her? Or is that pendant the only thing that matters to you?"

"If we don't retrieve that pendant, it won't matter if you save Thia or not. We will all be damned. You had better hope that Ruax does not find it before we do."

Vick extended his hand to my shoulder. I slapped it off and walked away from him.

"Lafayette. I am sorry. I should have told you more. But this isn't a time to dwell on that. We must find this pendant before Ruax does and then try to find Thia."

I slowly turned my gaze back to him. "And what if it's too late? Huh?"

"Then there is nothing more we can do."

"There is plenty we can do. You can go search for that pendant. I will search for Thia."

"What happens if you go in and can never return? You can't risk going in there on your own." Lee spoke up.

I slowly looked over at him and smiled. "I guess it's time that I find someone who will willingly go in for me."

"You are talking crazy, Lafayette. Are you seriously implying that you will create pawns to do your dirty work for you?" Vick scolded.

"Isn't that what you did? Isn't that what the order did? Don't try to press your moral convictions on me when you can't even abide by them yourself. Of course I will seek someone who can go into the portals for me, and damn it, I *will* get Thia back!"

I turned and began to walk away. Lee hurried to catch up with me. I felt him press his hand to my back and I stopped. Without turning around to look at him, I already knew what he would say.

"Wherever you go, my friend, I'll follow."

I turned to him and smiled, "I can always count on you."

I looked at the others and Vick shook his head in defeat.

"Who else is with me?" I added. The others stepped forward and Vick stayed behind.

"I will search for the pendant. You go find Thia." Vick shook his head.

I nodded and turned away from him and proceeded down the path of the unknown.

CHAPTER SEVEN
Mom

As night fell upon us, I couldn't stop thinking of Thia. I didn't know if she was even still alive. I just knew that I had to try to find her. This wasn't part of the mission. We were supposed to be searching for the watchers and eliminating them. Nothing was going according to plan anymore. I would have to devise a new one. I was beginning to get frustrated with this entire operation. I wanted to go home and just be as normal as I could for as long as I could. As my mind tried to focus on Thia, at the same time I was concerned about the pendant and wondered if I had made the right decision. *Could Ruax have found it by now?*

As I lay trying to go to sleep, my mind raced through one thing after another. Until this moment, I hadn't truly reflected on the event of meeting my father for the first time. All of the hatred I had built up over the years was amplified by his arrogance and spitefulness. Just as I had imagined all of my life, there was no love between us. I hated him even more now than ever. Somehow, I wanted to believe that he was lying and that he wasn't my father. Surely I couldn't have come from someone so evil. It was hard to imagine that he wasn't always evil. There was a time when he was loved and highly regarded by the gods. His jealousy and anger destroyed whatever good he ever possessed. I pitied him. The gods threw him away like garbage and forced him to live in such a savage and evil world. The darkness of this world is what made him transform into the monster that he became. Even still, he would destroy me if he had the chance. I just had to make sure that I destroyed him first.

I turned to see my friends all fast asleep. Lee lay on his back in the floor snoring like a hibernating bear. I laughed inside, remembering our sleepovers as kids and how even at a young age he could rumble the walls. Not much had changed with him except he was older and a little fatter. Somehow, he still seemed to harbor that youthfulness about him that just made him so easy to love. Of course, it was really hard to hate anyone that made me smile so much.

As for the others, I really wasn't sure about them, especially Asa. There was something unsettling about his eyes. They were black, but that wasn't unusual for his Asian ethnicity. It wasn't just his race that made his eyes appear dark. I couldn't quite put my finger on it. I just didn't trust him.

I lay watching everyone sleep and paid more attention to Asa. He didn't even sleep normal. He was turned over on his back with his arms crossed over his chest. He appeared to be dead. The rise and fall in his chest was the only thing that indicated he was very much alive.

I turned my attention to the ceiling. It was dimly lit by outside light, and an occasional passerby sent shadows casting eerily on its jagged surface. I wanted to sleep. I needed to sleep, but was too concerned about Thia to even give in to the notion of it. My heart ached to feel her close to me again. If only I knew that she was okay…

A scuffle outside of our room interrupted my thoughts. I turned my head towards the window. It was concealed by a heavy curtain that just barely reached the top, leaving about an inch of space that wasn't covered. Something felt amiss. An abrupt sense of panic consumed me and I lay paralyzed with fear.

I had become more and more paranoid since I arrived here and that wasn't like me. Typically I was very confident in my abilities to defend myself. This place had proven just how weak I was. I listened attentively and the scuffle began to sound more like pacing just outside of our door.

Carefully and quietly, I emerged from the bed and crept over to the window. I carefully pinched the fabric of the curtain in my fingers and slowly pulled back just enough to see outside. A figure stood looking the opposite direction of me as he draped his large body over the railing. I could see smoke bellowing out from the front of him and realized he was smoking a cigarette. I watched with great curiosity as to who this individual was lingering outside of our hotel room.

He turned facing the window and I quickly jumped back so as to not be seen. I pressed my back against the wall and breathed heavy as my heart pounded with fear. *Who is this person and what does he want?*

I heard footsteps approaching the door and I stood quietly hoping that he would just assume no one was in the room. I heard strange murmurings and realized someone else had joined the mysterious person. They spoke in a language that I was not familiar with and could only guess that it was some sort of European tongue. One voice was low and rather soft. The other was slightly higher pitched and very anxious sounding.

I stepped closer to the window again and peeked out. One stood with his back to me while the other faced him. He was in a position where the one with his back to me blocked the other man's face. I listened carefully trying to decipher their swift dialect, but it was of no use. It sounded like someone gargling while attempting to spit occasionally.

My eyes caught something glistening in the dim street lamps; something that hung around the other man's neck. It was a pendant that looked eerily similar to the one I so carelessly tossed away! Was it possible the pendant had been found? As I strained to see the details of the pendant I noticed that, while very similar to the one I had, it was slightly different. Mine possessed a quartz stone in it. This one possessed what looked like jade or an emerald. It reflected the small amount of light in a way that was almost blinding. If this was a pendant like mine, who was the one wearing it? What powers did it contain?

I had become so immersed in the idea of another pendant so close to us, and without any effort to conceal it, that I hadn't noticed the two men shake hands and part their own separate ways. It wasn't until the first man walked by my window, forcing me to jump back again, that I realized I had missed their entire interaction. I was intrigued to find out who they were, what they wanted, and why they wore a pendant so closely resembling mine.

For now, my questions would remain unanswered. I felt certain I would be seeing that man again really soon. I walked back to the bed. There were so many things going through my mind that I found it impossible to rest at all.

My mother was a popular girl in school. As captain of the cheer leading squad she could have her pick of any boy. She was really particular in the ones she would actually date. He had to be smart, he had to be popular, and he had to be blonde haired. It came as a shock when she began dating the awkward, shy, and academically challenged new kid. What was even stranger is that he also had beautiful long black hair, which completed his being a complete opposite of everything she wanted in a boy.

There was something about him that was alluring and captivating. She was instantly drawn in by his good looks and sweet disposition. He was a strange kid that didn't fit in to any social circle at school. He found a friend and much needed comfort in my mother.

He seemed to be a hit with my grandparents. They were also easily seduced by his good looks, manners, and charming attitude. He wasn't as far up on the social and economic ladder that my grandparents were, but they accepted him.

As they began to see more of each other, my mother fell deep in love with him and he seemed to share those feelings. Even though he came from just a typical middle class family, he always seemed to have money to shower her with extravagant gifts. On their three month anniversary he bought her a ring, while not very fancy she always cherished it. It was a silver ring with a white stone in it. He told her it was a symbol of his promise to her that he would never leave her.

On their six month anniversary he bought her a rare orchid in a beautiful pot and told her that their love was unique and beautiful. My grandparents fawned over his love for their daughter and warmly welcomed them into their home. When their one year anniversary came, he shocked everyone by buying her a new car. My grandparents questioned how a middle class teenager could afford such a thing and he told them that he had worked all year, saving money for a down payment, and would continue to make the payments on it. Again, though they found this somewhat peculiar, they didn't question.

A year and a half after they began dating my mother, who was now a senior in high school, had some devastating news. She had gotten pregnant.

Disappointed, my grandparents urged her to consider adoption, as she would have a more difficult time now going to college and succeeding in life. Her doting boyfriend convinced them that he would take care of her and her baby. They trusted him.

It was at that time Ruax explained to my mother that what she was carrying was indeed a special child. He told her that he was an angel and that her bloodline was of Enoch. My mother found this all hard to believe and as he explained further, her already being nephilim herself, her child would be something even greater and far more evil: a vampire.

This caused my mother to fall into depression where she doubted every word he told her. Somewhere in the back of her mind she must have wondered if it were true. She had heard stories like this in Sunday school, but she always brushed them off as fantastic fairy tales. Ruax decided to prove himself to her and exposed the darkness in his heart.

He caused himself to disappear before her eyes and then reappear. This terrified my mother even more so because he had returned with a young girl. As my mother watched, shocked and afraid, he slit the girl's throat. My mother screamed in horror and tried to run from him. He was too fast and caught her before she took more than a few steps. He filled his hand with the girl's blood and pressed it hard against my mother's abdomen. And from inside of her womb, I began to frantically try to claw my way out to get to the blood.

"You tell our son Daddy says hello when he's born." Then he disappeared with a fierce laugh.

The car he had bought for her was repossessed and she was faced with being a single mother without any financial help from him at all. She was determined she would succeed and be the best mother in the world. Even though she knew the creature inside of her would be immortal, I was still her son and she vowed to always love me and be

117

there for me as I transitioned into a creature of the night.

Months later, I arrived and she couldn't have been happier. I was born weighing eight pounds even. I was healthy and nothing seemed out of the ordinary. I was like any other baby. Her parents took care of me while mom went to a community college and earned a degree in business. From there she began work for a local company handling payroll. She was very happy with her job and finally making something of her life.

As I grew, the only noticeable difference in me compared to other kids my age was my extreme sensitivity to sunlight. She knew in her heart that what Ruax had told her was true. Nonetheless, she sought the advice of doctors who told her I had some sort of disease in my blood that prevented me from absorbing vitamin D properly. It wasn't fatal, but they warned my mother that I shouldn't be in the sun for more than ten minutes at a time and to always keep my skin covered. She knew that with me being what I was, the only thing she had to worry about was my taste for blood increasing.

The day I turned seven years old, she had planned a small birthday party for some friends and family to attend. She bought a cute cake with cars on it, decorated the house in a boyish car theme. Everything seemed to be going fine.

That evening friends and family gathered around me to sing happy birthday. When the song had ended everyone applauded as I blew out all of my candles. I heard a slow clap emerge from the back of the room. It was a stranger to me, but my mother and grandparents knew him. Shocked and dismayed to see him there, my mother demanded that he leave.

"Did you think I wouldn't be here to celebrate my son's seventh birthday?" He grinned as he approached where I sat at the table.

"You are no longer welcome at this house!" My grandfather sharply replied which set off an anger in my father that no one had ever seen.

His eyes lit up even more blue than before. His pale skin turned red with anger. Without warning he reached over me, grabbed my birthday cake, and threw it against the wall. As shock and fear washed over everyone in the house, my grandfather grabbed onto Ruax and shoved him against the wall.

People gasped and one woman screamed. As Ruax re-positioned himself for an attack my grandmother, who was normally very quiet and meek, grabbed a knife from the table and lunged towards him. Ruax kicked her in the chest and sent her flying across the room where she crashed into the counter on the other side of the table.

Grandma managed to cut her hand as she collided with the counter and small droplets of blood appeared on her skin. My eyes grew wide as a craving for blood shot through me. My mother quickly covered grandma's hand to lessen my desires and to make my true form less noticed by anyone else. She could see the black in my eyes and my skin turn a very pale gray color. For the first time ever, my own mother was afraid of me.

As everyone scrambled to check on grandma, my bizarre transformation was completely missed. Ruax made his exit without anyone noticing. My grandmother was a little bruised, cut, and shaken, but was otherwise okay.

Mom went the next day to file a restraining order against him, but that was the last anyone would see or hear from him.

A couple of years later my mom met and fell in love with a local real estate agent and they were married within a year. Their seemingly happy marriage soon fell to pieces when she discovered that he was cheating on her. As she prepared for a divorce, he became violent and started to vent his rage by hitting her.

He knew that a divorce would be very costly for him and he was not prepared to have to share his wealth with the woman that wanted nothing more to do with him. One night as we both slept, my step father came into a house that he was no longer living at, and attacked my mother. I heard her screams from my bedroom and I quickly emerged from my bed to see what the problem was.

I ran into her bedroom and saw him on top of her on the bed pounding his fist into her face repeatedly. She tried with all her might to fight back, but she was no match for this man who was nearly twice her size.

I quickly ran to them and jumped on his back. I began to beat his head with my fists. He grabbed onto me and tried to pull me off. That was when something inside of me exploded and I felt an energy I had never felt before. Without understanding why or how, I pressed my mouth into his neck and dug my teeth into his flesh. He let out a

119

horrified scream as his blood began to fill my mouth.

My mother, realizing what I had done, scrambled to pull me off of him. I kept a firm latch and continued to feast on his delicious blood. He struggled to get away from me. The harder he fought, the deeper I embedded my teeth into him.

My mother managed to completely free herself from under his fighting body and pulled me off of him. He fell to the floor holding his neck and screaming. My mother took me by the hand and quickly pulled me out of the house and into our car where we immediately went to the police station to file a report.

From that day on, I knew that I was different than everyone else. Mom tried to conceal me from the world as much as she could, but she knew I had to go to school and live as normal of a life as I possibly could.

She made me promise her that I would learn to control my urges and to not hurt anyone. If my desire for blood became too great, she would take me into the woods and slaughter a rabbit or some other small creature for me to drink from. For my mother's sake, I swore that I wouldn't hurt another human to meet my needs. In time I did learn to control it. I grew much stronger over the years and learned to live as a normal human.

All of this took a toll on my mother. After a mental break down and suicide attempt, she was admitted into a psychiatric facility. I was, for once in my life, alone. Mom never fully explained to me WHAT my father was and I always assumed that I had gotten my rare gifts from him. I had no idea that my mother was special as well.

From age twelve, my grandparents cared for me until I was old enough to make it in the world alone. I left home and never looked back. It has been so long since I saw my mother or grandparents, I didn't even know if any of them were even still alive.

I did often wonder about my mom. Did she even think of me anymore? If she were still alive, has she ever tried to find me? With a name like Lafayette de Bucci, it wouldn't be too hard.

土

As I lay in bed, my thoughts racing from one thing to another, they went to Thia. During our short time together and realizing how important she was to me, I couldn't ever imagine my life without her. As those thoughts entered my head, I was forced to realize that for now I was without her. This was forbidden. If a child were born from this outlawed relationship, he or she would be hunted and killed. This concerned me even though we hadn't yet reached that level in our relationship.

I knew it was only a matter of time before that happened. I didn't want to hurt her. More importantly, I didn't want to bring another demon child into this sick and evil world. It became funny to me how we were inherently evil just for being born demons. After all, it wasn't my kind slaughtering innocent people all over the world and destroying everything that breathed. We were supposed to be the monsters. Yet here I was trying to save these filthy humans from the evil they had helped create.

And my mother, who was innocent, was dragged into this as well. She didn't ask for her ancestors to mingle with the "bad seed" and bear a child even more wicked. I didn't ask to be born of this nature.

As I pondered my existence and all that had happened before my time, I wondered why the gods would allow such a thing to happen. What did they get out of all this pain? I longed to approach those gods and ask them why they created humans if they would become so evil, immoral, and corrupt. I also wanted to learn more about who I was. Not my human side, but the demon inside of me that damned me at conception. Without a human soul, what would happen to me when I died?

Feeling somewhat frustrated with things I had no hand in nor could control, I huffed and rolled over in the bed to see Asa lying there on the floor staring at me. I was a bit startled at first because his eyes were wide and bright.

"Asa?" I scooted closer to the edge of my bed.

In an instant his eyes shifted from a wide nervous look back to a normal stare. It was as if he was in a trance and my voice had awakened him.

"Can't sleep either?" he whispered.

"Someone was just outside of our door." I turned to look in the direction the two men had been.

"Who were they?"

"I'm not sure, but one of them wore a pendant much like the one I had."

"Do you think they are one of the watchers?"

I sighed. "I have no idea. Something about them just made me really nervous. Why were they standing outside of our room? Were they looking for me?"

"There are a lot of strange things happening Lafayette, things we can't explain. Whatever this is, we will figure it out and we'll help you get your girlfriend back."

My stomach knotted up at the mention of Thia being my girlfriend. I was still trying to process it myself.

"Yeah about that. Don't go around telling anyone. We're kind of not allowed to do that."

"Says who?"

"The order. They make the rules."

"Sounds like a stupid rule to me. They can't tell you who you can or can't fall in love with."

"Well actually, they can. They seem to think that we aren't supposed to have any feelings or desires outside of being their slaves; most of the time that isn't even an issue. Most vampires aren't actively seeking people to settle down and grow old with. For a vampire to physically mingle with a human is forbidden. To mingle with an angel is a death sentence. If they knew of me and Thia..." I paused and turned my attention back to the window. Something felt strange and out of place. My heart began to pound and my breathing increased.

"Lafayette?" Asa whispered in a concerned tone.

I placed my finger to my lips and continued to listen for the disturbance I could feel outside. Slowly and quietly I left the bed and proceeded back to the window. As I gently pulled the corner of the curtain just a bit, I saw a face in the window starring back at me. It was dark and soulless. The second its eyes caught mine, it snarled and let out a piercing cry. I jumped back with my hand over my heart and breathed so fast I thought I would hyperventilate.

"What is it?" Asa ducked low on his cot.

I quickly and quietly ran over to him and ducked down on the other side of my bed.

"I don't know, but it saw me this time." I could still hear its loud shrieks and I covered my ears to muffle the sounds.

"What? Lafayette, what's going on?"

I looked up at Asa with a grimacing look and pressed my hands harder to my ears.

"You don't hear that?"

"Hear what?"

It was obvious that whatever was outside, I seemed to be the only one that could hear its cries. It sounded like some poor soul in the deepest and most tormenting realm of Hell crying out in agony. Even in all of the sounds of terror and pain I could feel something reaching out to me, tugging at me to come closer. Against my better judgment, I rose from where I crouched and crept to the window once again. I pressed my ear against the curtain and listened. The shrill sounds were deafening and physically painful.

By now the disturbance in the room had awakened everyone else. They sat up and stared at me, wondering what was going on.

"Lafayette what—," Lee began. I put my finger to my lips again and everyone grew quiet and appeared rather nervous. I slowly pulled back the curtain again. This time I wasn't face to face with some demon. I was hit with a blinding flash of light. I covered my eyes and then, all at once, the screams disappeared. It was eerily quiet.

I slowly removed my hands from my face and found myself in the middle of an open field. The sky was clear blue and the sun was shining brightly. I looked down at my hands and they appeared normal. There was no indication of my demon form showing and I wondered what sort of alternate reality I was in.

At the top of a hill in front of me was a large tree that stood strong and proud. It did not look like any tree I had ever seen before. Its leaves were long and wispy, like a willow. It held more of a lavender color and it gave off an inviting glow. It was breathtakingly beautiful.

Standing beside the tree and facing away from me was a woman. I felt a sense of peace come over me. I slowly began to make my way toward the top of the hill.

"Hello?" I called out to the mysterious being.

She just stood and continued looking in the opposite direction.

As I neared the tree, the woman slowly turned around. My eyes grew wide and my mouth hung open when I recognized her.

"Momma?"

She smiled gently and said nothing as I slowly moved closer to her.

"Where am I? Where is this place? How did you get here?"

She slowly turned her head to the tree and put one of her fragile looking hands against its trunk.

"This is the oldest tree in existence; even older than some of the angels. Within it lies the fate of every human on this planet." Her voice was soft and gentle.

"The Tree of Life?" I stood beside her, touching the tree with my hand and marveling at its incredible beauty.

"The tree most sought after by angels; the one flaw in the creation of the gods. If they are able to gather enough souls they can pass through the portal of time and obtain access to the tree of life. With it, they shall receive eternal life in the heavens with the gods. This is something we cannot allow to happen." She turned her stare towards the sky and sighed deeply.

"You must not let Ruax get the pendants, Lafayette. With it, he plans to unleash Azazel from his earthly prison and seek the tree so that he can obtain all the power and knowledge of the gods. He will then destroy everyone on this planet, including you."

She turned to look at me, her brown eyes heavy with pain and sorrow, "A war is coming. Unlike any this world has ever seen. Only you can stop it."

"How? Momma, I don't know what to do."

My eyes filled with tears. She lovingly placed her hand on my cheek. "Oh my son, I knew the day you were born that you'd become someone very special. Though you're a product of abomination, the gods have favored you over all other creatures of the night. They know that your heart is pure and strives for goodness in this world. Even as that gives you strength, it is also your weakness. You are as much human as you are demon and that gives you compassion and love, something that most vampires lack."

"How do I defeat this darkness?" I was feeling overwhelmed by her presence and all that she was telling me.

"Lafayette, you need to forget about Thia. She served her mission for the time that she was here. From now on, your only mission is to find the pendants, destroy this evil plague stretching all across the world, and restore humanity to what it was intended to be before the angels corrupted and scarred them."

"Forget Thia? I can't do that, Mom. I love her."

"Oh Lafayette, that's how you are weak. You can't let anyone stand in the way of you completing this mission and saving humanity."

I gritted my teeth with anger, not towards her directly, but to the idea that I should even consider abandoning Thia. My heart would never forgive me for it.

"Forget her, my son. Do what you were put here to do. The gods will reward you in ways you haven't even thought of. Forget everything the order instructed you to do and just find these pendants. Keep them safe. Be warned, when the four of them are combined, within them will be a power that you have never known. I pray you have the strength to wield it, its power is that of the gods. If you are not strong, my son, it will defeat you and draw you into the darkness of evil for eternity."

I sighed realizing this mission just became a lot harder and much more stressful. I didn't even know if I wanted the task anymore.

"Where do I find the pendants? Where is the one I so carelessly tossed away?"

She smiled as she reached around her neck, clasping a gold chain. Then she held out her hands to me and in it was the pendant that I had tossed into the portal. My eyes were wide with astonishment.

"But how—."

"Never be so careless with it again. The rest of these you will find in the hands of angels and men. They are kept by those who were trusted to guard the pendants and their secrets at all cost. The watchers and their army are searching for you. They were ordered to kill you. You must be safe and destroy them before they can get to you. And remember this, my son, no matter how tempting it is, you must never drink the blood of these wicked men. They are tainted and corrupt and will corrupt you as well. Eliminate them, but do not feast on their tainted blood. If you can get back the pendants, destroy these wicked men, and resist the temptation of your dark side the gods will reward you."

I tried to digest all that she had just told me. My mind was screaming that it had to be done, but my heart only thought of Thia.

"You see this tree?" Her question snapped me out of my thoughts and I nodded.

"This tree is a promise for all who seek its wisdom. It represents eternal life to those who aren't blinded by the greed of this world. Even you, Lafayette, it's here for you as well."

"I don't have a human soul." I corrected her.

She looked up high in the tree and grinned wide.

"A soul is something that chooses you. When we're born, we don't automatically come with a soul. A free soul decides the human vessel it will inhabit for whatever particular reasons. The soul within you chose you because it felt that you are strong and capable of completing this task."

I felt somewhat at ease and hopeful for a moment, but there was still the issue with Thia. I knew in my heart that I could not abandon her. I wouldn't tell my mother any more about my reservations. I wondered if she was telling the truth and that there was hope for me having a soul.

"We must part for now. My time here has ended and my time on Earth ended a long time ago. We will meet again, I promise."

She turned and began to walk away from me, stopping only to look back and mouth the words, "I love you."

As she drifted off towards the setting sun, I tried to follow. My steps seemed slow, like I was barely moving. I reached out for her and began to cry as she disappeared.

I fell to the ground and wept as the feeling became too intense for me to bear. I buried my face in my hands and cried until I felt my heart was empty. When I lifted my hands from my face, I was back in the dark room surrounded by my friends.

I was in a state of shock and disorientation. I had no idea what had just happened and if it had all just been a dream. It felt real, all of it; Mom's hand on my cheek, the tears burning as they fell from my eyes, and the amazing sight of that beautiful tree.

"Oh thank God you are okay!" Lee grabbed onto me in a tight bear hug.

"What happened?" I looked around at the others.

"You opened the curtain and then you fainted. A few seconds later, you came to."

I was puzzled. The place I had been was either a dream or it was not of this world. How much time had lapsed without the others even realizing.

"I don't know what happened, but there was a bright flash of light and then..." I paused to reflect on what had just happened and I felt disoriented and confused.

"I saw my mother. She warned me of what is to come and..." I held out my hand revealing the pendant.

Vick rose up from behind everyone, shocked to see the pendant in my hand again.

"You were only out for a few seconds," Asa scoffed.

"He was in a time portal." We all tuned towards Vick as he spoke.

"You were in a time portal, which means that time continued

for you, but stopped for us. You say you saw your mother, what did she tell you?" Vick continued.

"Well, pretty much what you and Ruax said. We must find those pendants and keep them out of his hands. Oh God my head hurts!" I winced and grabbed my head. I had been having more headaches lately and wasn't sure why. It wasn't normal for vampires to ever get sick.

"How did you get the pendant?" Vick walked slowly toward me as he spoke.

"Mom gave it to me. Don't ask me she got it. I just have it and that's all that matters. She told me where the others are. I mean, not specifically, but it's humans and angels that have them... powerful beings. The only way to obtain them myself is to convince the humans to give them to me, which won't be easy. They are addicted to the powers that the pendants possess. Mom said the gods are confident that I can do this, though I don't think I can."

"Did she tell you anything else?" Vick probed me for more.

I didn't want to tell him what she said about Thia because then they would all gang up on me and try to convince me that she was a lost cause. I was not about to have to fight my way out of their lack of understanding. I knew at some point I would have to leave my friends behind and continue this mission on my own. As much as they tried to help, they were more of a hindrance to me now. Lee and the others would still be useful in hacking into government databases, for now, I felt that this mission was mine and mine alone.

CHAPTER EIGHT
The Second Pendant

The darkness had started to become familiar and the sounds of the dead no longer seemed to bother her. Thia was bored and sick of not being able to do the things that she enjoyed.

Ruax was standing in the same spot that he had occupied many times before, watching the humans and the rest of the demons interact. He seemed depressed and somewhat lonely and there seemed to be a longing to be like those who just enjoyed life without the constant restraints of being non-human. His face twisted in rage and he threw something across the room, yelling out in frustration. Thia didn't flinch. She had grown used to his tantrums.

"Seriously, how long are you going to keep me here?" she continued, observing his restless behavior.

"Until your boyfriend comes to his senses and sorts out his priorities."

"You're just mad that you couldn't break him."

Ruax stopped abruptly with his back facing her and slammed his fist against the stone wall in front of him.

"You sure do talk a lot for someone that is being held against their will."

"Yeah, well you're not the only person to ever say that to me. Certainly won't be the last. You aren't going to get him to bend. Not even for me. He knows what's most important."

Ruax sighed and returned to the image of the outside world.

"For millennia we have searched for those pendants. We have come close to finding them, but they change hands so much. From the native tribes in the Americas, the Aztecs, those blasted Hebrews that we just can't seem to break, and half of the Middle East. We tried to seduce them with gold and oil and that still didn't work."

"Maybe because the will of man is much stronger than you thought."

Ruax turned to face her. *"We cause them to turn on each other. We bomb their countries into oblivion. We starve them and yet they still cling to hope as if it's still alive for them."*

"You did this, all of it. Your jealousy and greed is destroying this world, but you can't destroy the spirits of man. What does that tell you, Ruax? You won't win. No matter how hard you try. No matter how much you destroy this world, mankind will always salvage the bits and pieces and put it all back together again."

Ruax sighed and leaned in towards the stone wall. It was obvious that he was growing even more frustrated.

"Humans are weak. They put their faith in their man-made religions and fake gods in hopes they will save them. They have to have leaders and masters to tell them what to do and think because they lack the ability to do so themselves. They divide themselves by race, gender, and beliefs. Those are the very things that will destroy them."

"How long have you and your kind been trying to break them? For thousands of years you have been on this quest to bring the humans to their knees. They always bounce back. Give up already. The gods threw you out because of your jealousy and rage. Just stop already. You were defeated the day you arrived here."

He slowly turned to face her, his lips tightly drawn to his teeth and his face flustered.

"Then I guess I will have to turn up the heat a bit. How would your precious lover react if I start sending him bits and pieces of you?"

Thia gulped in fear, but refused to let him know that his words had stirred her even in the slightest.

"You do what you have to do. Whatever you do to me, he will never break."

"You are so certain. We will see." He brushed his hand against the image of the outside world and it disappeared.

As everyone began to wake the next day, I knew that I had to leave without them and began thinking of a plan. I knew Vick wouldn't let me just wander out alone, but I had to. I needed to figure this out on my own.

"Hey guys, I think I'll go for a walk and clear my head," I said as I got dressed. They all looked up at me as if to question my motives.

"I don't think it's a good idea for you to venture out on your own, Lafayette," Vick reminded me.

I turned to face him. "Yeah, well, I don't think you should really give your advice to me anymore considering everything you have ordered me to do has failed miserably."

"Did I not advise you and Thia to stay in the hotel room that day? You cannot blame me for any of this. I told you what was out there and neither of you listened to me! Your humanity is going to destroy you. I think it's time that you realize who and what you are and stop pretending that you're human. Be the demon you were created to be, find your inner powers, and *do* something about this!"

"Great then. I will find my inner demon out there while I'm draining the life out of some poor soul." I had no intentions of doing that. I just wanted to point out just how evil and ruthless I could be.

"That isn't how you prove yourself to the gods, Lafayette," Vick scolded.

"Well maybe I have nothing to prove to them anymore. Where have they been my entire miserable life? Eh?"

I glared at him and for a brief moment. I wanted to remind him that I never invited him on this mission. I never asked for his help or his concern. I decided that it would be pointless to argue. I grabbed my coat and sunglasses and gave them a final look.

"Don't follow me. I want to be alone. Lee, you and the others just keep doing what you do best. Try to find out more information on what these government idiots are planning. I will get back with you all later."

I proceeded to the door where Vick quickly intercepted me.

"Please reconsider this. We are a team and we must stick together."

"I've never been a part of any team. I've always been alone and done well my entire life. I will figure this out on my own. Get out of my way." I slapped his hand away from the door. He didn't try to stop me again as I walked out.

The sun was unusually bright today. I knew that I was taking a huge risk by being out in it, but for once I didn't care. I had to figure out what to do.

As I made my way down the sidewalk, trying to shield myself from the glaring sun, I wondered where exactly I was going. I had no idea what I was doing anymore. My heart weighed heavily on the thoughts of Thia, my asshole father, and my mother. She had told me that her time on this Earth had ended long ago. I didn't even know she had passed away. Not that anyone at the center would have had any way to contact me. I didn't even talk to my grandparents anymore. I felt all alone in this world.

As I strolled down the sidewalk, my head deep in thought, something caught my attention out of the corner of my eye. I stopped and took note of a shop with some weird writing on it, like ancient Egyptian hieroglyphics or something. It smelled strong of incense and there was something alluring about it. I proceeded to walk into the shop.

It wasn't well lit. Mixed with the strong aromas was some strange soft music playing in the background. I looked at the many artifacts displayed. Some just appeared to be over priced old junk. As I slowly made my way to the counter, one item instantly caught my attention.

A pendant similar to mine was hanging behind a display case. It looked very much like the one I had seen the night before when those strangers congregated by our window. I was so enthralled I didn't notice an old man approached me until he spoke.

"Good day, sir. What can I do for you?" The old man's voice held a thick Irish accent.

"This pendant, how much is it?"

"Oh, it's not for sale. It's been in my family for centuries."

"You don't say?" I observed its markings, much like mine. This one bore a green stone in the center, but the markings were the same as the one I had except the lines were drawn in different directions.

"Can you tell me anything about it? I am curious because..." I reached into my pocket and retrieved my own pendant.

The old man's eyes grew large. He grabbed on to me arm and began to pull. "Quickly, we must go somewhere private."

He turned to the display case, opened it and pulled out the other pendant. He ushered me to a back room where he quickly closed the door.

"Where did you get that?" His eyes seemed to blaze.

"You wouldn't believe me if I told you."

He leaned in close to me and whispered, "Try me!"

I sighed and clutched the pendant tightly in my hand. "There are more of these, aren't there?"

"According to what my ancestors believed, there are four. Each one representing the four elements of the earth: fire, water, air and earth. When combined they become very powerful."

"Do you know where the other pendants are?"

"It's not known. Each one was entrusted with different families over the centuries. I hear tell they are with secluded and secretive families or religious groups. No one really knows where the others are. It is the secret that has protected them for so long. If no one knows where they are, the ones that seek them will not find them."

"And who seeks them?"

The man seemed troubled by my questions and acted hesitant to give up info easily.

"I need to know this. I am in great danger. And so is all of mankind," I pleaded.

He looked so deep into my eyes it made me slightly uncomfortable.

"You aren't human, are you?"

Somewhat shocked and growing increasingly nervous, I stammered trying to find words to speak.

"Don't worry, your secret's safe with me. There's a prophecy that was handed down from generation to generation that spoke of a chosen one, a being that wasn't entirely human nor entirely spiritual. He would lead an army of mortals and immortals to defeat the evil which had been brought to this earth in the beginning of creation."

"I don't know if I am *the* chosen one, but I have been cursed with the task of taking out the watchers. Are you familiar with them?"

The old man sighed and appeared a bit troubled by my question.

"That is such a great burden to bear, Lafayette."

My eyes grew wide. *How did he know my name??*

"How'd you—."

"It's in your eyes. Your soul is dark, but you yearn for light. You're no stranger to those who await your coming. For centuries, mankind has tried to destroy the evil, not fully understanding exactly what it was they were fighting against. There are a few that are waking up and obtaining full knowledge of the gods. Sadly, so many of them are dying at a swift and unprecedented rate."

He held his pendant in his hand and placed it next to mine. Immediately, the two seemed to be communicating with each other. They vibrated in unison and their stones began to glow brightly.

"They have waited so long for this day, to be unified with each other. The one that you possess is the element of earth. The one in my hand is the element of air. Combined they can control the weather and the growth which sustains life on Earth. In the wrong hands, you will see famine start to consume the world. The weather will begin to turn on creation and destroy everything in its path. You must not let the one who seeks it obtain it. You must guard them with your life."

"What happens once all pendants are together?" Even though

this had been explained to me before by Vick and my mother, I wanted to hear what this wise old man had to say about it.

"Then the one that possesses them will control the four elements and mankind's fate."

Very much what Vick and my mother told me.

"I am a vampire born from the blood line of Enoch. My mission is to destroy the fallen angels and restore humanity to what it was intended. And I cannot do this without the pendants. I must have that one."

The old man looked into my eyes, his fragile worn down cheeks tightening with a smile that he struggled to produce. He placed one hand below mine and his other on top.

"You are the one chosen for these stones. My task in guarding it is now over. You alone have the power to use these stones to save mankind. Be careful Lafayette, in your possession these stones are activated and their powers can become very destructive. Be mindful of what can happen now that you have them both. It's not going to be pretty, but in the end, it will save us."

"What do you mean they are activated?"

"In your hands these pendants begin to react and each element becomes greatly affected by it. Ruax is seeking the pendants for his own personal gain. There is one more item that he is not aware of, something that will control the pendants if all are found."

I was amazed at this old man's knowledge of my mission and the ones I was seeking; more so his understanding of the pendants and their power.

"There is a locket that you must find. The watchers are not aware of this. It holds each pendant making it even more powerful and potentially destructive. Ruax plans to use these pendants to unleash the foulest and most evil being ever created from his prison. Without the locket, he will never be able to achieve this."

I sighed, briefly feeling elated that Ruax wouldn't have much control without the locket. However, this posed another important question.

"So where do I find this locket?"

"This I cannot tell you. It's not clear who originally possessed it or who has it now. I wager that the one who entrusted it to its source knew that the person would have to be completely immune to its power and not try to use it for evil. That the person would somehow give it to you some day."

"And what will I do with it once I have it?"

"You must protect it with your life."

Well that shouldn't be too difficult since I was THE chosen one. This task just took a different turn of events that I was not sure how to embrace. It was a lot to take in. Not only did I need to find the rest of the pendants, but also the locket. I had no idea where it was or even how to begin searching for it. I wanted to find Thia and I seemed to be completely alone in that. Eventually, it would just be me to complete this and I was not prepared for all that was coming.

"Well, thank you. I don't know how you knew of me or the mission, but I am glad that I stumbled across you. What's your name? I didn't catch it."

The old man cleared his throat and looked deeply into my eyes.

"Gabriel. Just call me Gabriel."

As I left the shop, my heart was heavy with the burden of my new task. I didn't even want the first one and now I would have to find two more as well.

As I walked, I was suddenly struck with intense pain in my head. I grabbed my head with both hands as my eyes clamped shut. The pain forced me to stop dead in my tracks and fall to the ground. I slowly opened my eyes to see everything around me spinning. Without warning the sun, which was usually hidden behind clouds here, began to emerge with bright and painful rays. I felt so overwhelmed with nausea and agony that I became completely disoriented.

I heard deafening screams and shrills sounding in the sky. I could not pin point its exact location or source. No one else around me seemed effected by any of it. It was clear to me that I was in great danger, but with the sun's rays beaming down on me I was rendered completely incapacitated.

My eyes were shut tightly again, my hands squeezing the side of my head, and then I felt a sudden and powerful kick to my jaw. I fell backwards with my hands now resting to the side of my head and the sunlight piercing through my immortal flesh. The creature that attacked me quickly moved on top of me, pinning me down to the ground and began to slam his fist repeatedly into my skull. I felt weak and unable to fight back and with each blow I fell deeper and deeper into an almost unconscious state. I could taste my own blood gushing from my wounds and the life draining from my body.

With my eyes closed and on the brink of passing out, I could hear a commotion around me that sounded like multiple voices. I opened my eyes to see what was going on, but the sun was blinding me. All I could make out were dark, blurred images of several figures. I hoped they were people. I felt the creature being pulled off of me and then a hand reach into my pocket where the pendant was stored. I tried to fight against it but to no avail. In a flash, I found myself in a familiar place, Vick's magical box.

The sunlight was gone and I could make out the faces of my friends standing before me. Lee rushed to my side and lifted me into an upright position as the others quickly surrounded me.

"Oh my God! Lafayette, are you okay?" Lee frantically asked.

I was still dazed and somewhat confused as I tried to regain my focus and strength.

"Yeah. I think so. What was that?" I was rubbing the side of my head, revealing a terrible and very bloody wound.

Vick approached me and pressed a handkerchief to the wound firmly to stop the bleeding.

"That was a bad ass demon of sorts," Asa said.

"How was it you could see it but no one else around me could?" I winced in the pain that talking caused.

"No one else saw it?" Lee stared at me wide eyed.

I looked up at him and then at Vick who seemed equally confused.

"They didn't appear to know what was going on. At least, that's what I gathered shortly before the sun came out and then I couldn't see anything."

"Perhaps the only ones who can see the demons are those who believe in them." Vick said offering what seemed to be a logical explanation.

"Yeah, like this shit hole isn't aware of the demons that run this place. AH! My head is killing me!" The throbbing pain continued getting more severe by the second.

"We need to get you back to the hotel and treat that wound. It's pretty nasty," Lee said as Vick attempted to wipe the blood that was now flowing down the side of my face.

"Wow, vampire blood looks so… human-like." Lee chuckled, trying to defuse the tension of the situation. I quickly raised my middle finger to him and mockingly laughed.

"Luckily we were there to save your ass again." Asa crouched down beside me.

Vick then held up both pendants with his other hand and shot me a questioning look.

"Where did you get this?" He asked referring to the new pendant.

"Some old man in a shop I came across. He was very knowledgeable in our mission. He even knew my name."

"And what was his name?" Vick's gaze seemed to bore right into my chest.

I thought for a moment as it had briefly escaped my mind.

"I can't remember. Greg? Garrett?" I began to recite off similar names.

"Gabriel." I heard Vick whisper.

"Yeah. Gabriel. Do you know him?"

Vick sighed and smiled slightly.

"There isn't a being mortal or otherwise that doesn't know Gabriel. What did he say to you?"

"He said a lot; something about a locket and Azazel. Hell, I can't remember right now. My head hurts too much to think. I need some damn food. That creature wouldn't have whipped my ass if I got some decent nourishment once in a while."

"I think it's time to introduce you to my friend Evan. He can help with that. I do agree that you must maintain your strength because these attacks will come more often, now that you have two pendants." Vick hung his head.

I tried to stand, but felt instantly light headed and plopped back to the ground in a heap. Vick put his hand on my shoulder to force me to stay down.

"Don't stand. Not yet. You are weak and have lost a lot of blood. When we are able to get back to the hotel I want you to get some proper sleep then we will decide what to do from there. I want to know more about this locket and then we can figure out how to find Thia."

I looked up at Vick with a rather pitiful look on my face. He was finally ready to look for Thia, which I was greatly relieved for.

"I thought you wanted to forget about her."

"No. We can never forget our Thia, but I need you to focus on the task at hand. It's obvious that you are increasingly distracted with worry over her. So it's best if we find her so that you can focus on the mission again."

I felt my body start to grow numb and I was very tired. I think I passed out. Or fell asleep. Or maybe I just succumbed to the hunger and my body shut down.

CHAPTER NINE
Return of Thia

Thia was growing ever wearier of being held captive. She would have to come up with a clever plan if she would be released from her prison. Ruax seemed to gaze into his vision portal more often lately and seemed ever more restless. Thia, on the other hand, was bored out of her mind.

"You said that you could release Azazel, correct?"

He tuned slowly to face her with a curious look on his face.

"Once I have all of the pendants, I can use their powers to destroy the mountain where he's a prisoner at. Then he will finally be free."

"Well, as angry as this situation makes me, I'm willing to help you if you promise me that I will be reunited with him in the end."

"I'm listening." Ruax took the bait.

"I can convince Lafayette to hand over the pendants to you, but you have to promise me that you won't hurt him. Just let him be. He suffers enough just being a creature of the damned. No need to punish him further."

"Oh Thia, for an angel you sure do have the empathy of a human. I can promise you that if your dear Lafayette willingly gives me the pendants, I will inflict no further harm on his miserable existence. I think you put it best, 'as a creature of mixed race, he has no place in Heaven or Hell.' That alone brings me much joy. So how will you convince him to hand over the pendants?"

"Leave that to me. I'm a smart girl. Just get me Azazel. That's all I have longed for since I was cursed to this wretched planet."

Ruax smiled devilishly, thinking that he had finally won. For now, Thia wouldn't allow him to believe anything to the contrary.

I was tired of dreaming. I was tired of existing in this world. Thia was right in that I did envy humans. Their time in this world was limited and they drew comfort in knowing that they would die someday. For me, death was a much more complicated task.

I was tired. I felt broken. More so, I was just sick of humans. I was sick of their greed, their hatred towards one another, their sick and perverse desire to control one another, and using great evil to carry out their will. Why the gods favored them over my kind was beyond any comprehension.

They were a flawed creation right from the start. The moment the gods gave them free will they also gave them the right to choose it. This had led to the down fall of man. I didn't feel there was a way to save such a damned race, but I had to keep with the mission to do so.

What was in it in the end for me? Nothing. I didn't have the promise of eternal life after leaving this world. I didn't get to choose which god would get me there. I realized that I was nothing more than a puppet and my existence didn't matter one bit. Oh, how I had grown to hate them. Their precious, spoiled and rebellious human children were destroying everything the gods had worked hard to create. And yet, the gods still loved them. Why were they so special?

I stood in the center of a black room illuminated only by small fractals of lights that seemed to have no origin or reason to exist, I watched as the four pendants floated around me. Like long lost lovers finally reunified, they slowly danced around me. A locket with four symmetric triangles, one on each corner appeared, in a flash of light and gravitated towards the center of the pendants. They almost seemed overjoyed at the newcomer.

As I watched the pendants moved in towards the locket and, one by one, they fitted themselves inside its spaces. When the first one was locked in, I felt the ground shake. As the second and third pendants took their place I heard what sounded like thunder and then the sounds of a crashing wave. Finally, as the last pendant implanted itself inside of the locket, the room filled with an intense inferno that lit up brighter than the sun.

The heat was so intense that I felt it burn my skin. I didn't fully comprehend what was happening, but I knew that I was in the possession of something very powerful. As I reached out to, it almost appeared to leap towards my grip willingly, as if it belonged there and had waited for centuries to find its way there. Once clutched securely in my palm, I could feel its power at work. It was coursing through every fiber of my being. It felt so good, rejuvenating, and empowering. Inside of this nothingness that had engulfed me, I could hear voices screaming in agony. Tormented souls, damned for all of eternity, lamenting at my achievement.

Just as quickly as all that had unfolded before me, I found myself outside in an open field. The sun was shining brightly. I could smell the fresh scent of wild flowers growing nearby and heard the whistling and chirping of birds. I could see the tree of life and once again a figure was standing near it. Only this time, it wasn't my mother. It was the old man that I had met at the shop who gave me the second pendant.

As I approached him, he seemed fully aware of my presence.

"Beautiful, isn't she?" He smiled at the old tree.

I just nodded and hummed an acknowledgment.

"Funny how this thing is the cause of so much pain right now isn't it? All they want is to become human so that the gods will love them again." He reached out and rested a hand on the ancient trunk.

He turned to me with a grin on his face, "Which would sound really sad if they weren't so wicked. You can understand their desires, as you have felt them yourself. What sets you a part from them is your humanity. You can empathize with humans without allowing your envy and rage to consume you and turn you into the monster they would like to believe you are."

He turned back to the tree and took in a deep breath. "Ah, the air is so nice here. I haven't been able to breathe this well in so long."

He looked back at me, his eyes shining. "Before long, Lafayette, the humans will accept you and grow to love you. Eventually the gods will also come to their senses and realize that, even though you were created out of a forbidden act, you are still a good person that deserves their love just like the humans. In the end, everything that you have done will be recognized and you will finally have what it is you want. I feel certain Thia will as well."

I perked up at the sound of her name coming from his lips.

"Thia? Is she okay?"

"She is more than okay. She is tough Lafayette, probably tougher than you give her credit for. She has endured a great deal of suffering at the hand of Ruax. The gods can't wait to get their vengeance on him. He has defied all orders from them and they are not pleased. Thia will return to you very soon, but you must take heed in all that she has to say. Do not doubt her for one second. Trust in her. Trust in your love for her. Never leave her side for as long as you both remain on Earth."

My eyes filled with tears. I was once again hopeful that I would be seeing Thia very soon. The emotion had really begun to get to me when I felt the old man's hand touch my shoulder.

"Your love is a forbidden one, but so has been every great love story ever told. It's that defiance and will that makes love between two beings that more beautiful. In time the gods will approve of your union and bless it. But for now, don't worry about that at all. It's not important. What is important is that you find the pendants and the locket and keep them safe. Destroy as many of the watchers and their pawns as you can and soon it will all be over. The journey ahead will be a dangerous and painful one; never falter. Be strong and courageous, Lafayette. Anytime that you are in doubt or certain that you just don't know what to do, call on me and I will be there. We archangels are depending on you to set this straight once and for all."

Archangel? Of course, it made sense now. That is how he knew who I was and how he knew to entrust me with the second pendant.

As his voice trailed off to a whisper, I suddenly found myself standing before another being. This one I didn't recognize.

"You must hurry Lafayette. The watchers are fast approaching to gain access to the pendants and attempt to unleash the foulest beast ever created from his dungeon. They need him to get to the tree of life. You must stop them!"

Another being appeared and added, "The world elites are in a fast pace to completely dismantle humanity. The wars are going to get much worse. Using their own weather modification programs to change the climate; DNA tampering that will alter humanity and poisoning the food; they are sure to succeed unless you step in and stop them!"

The voices began to overlap one another and the information they were giving was too much to take in at once. *Weather modification? DNA tampering? Why would the watchers even be interested in such things?*

By now I couldn't distinguish one voice from another and it was deafening. I covered my ears as they all shouted at me to stop this global terror from happening. I couldn't take the chaos and the noise. I screamed at the top of my lungs, "GO AWAY!"

I opened my eyes to find myself lying in an unfamiliar bed with Lee sitting in a chair beside me. His head was in his hands and he almost looked like he was praying. It seemed a bit comical for me since I was certain prayers didn't work on my kind.

I rolled to my side, which alerted him to my awakening.

"Lafayette, oh thank God! You're finally awake." He leaned in close to me.

"Where am I?" I looked down at an IV line running through my arm, "What is this?"

"Be still. That's a blood IV. You were so malnourished that the doc had to hook you up to one. You are feeding off the best and purest blood there is."

"The doc? What doc? Where's Vick and the others?"

"Doc is a friend of Vick's. You're at his house. He works in the hospital and has access to a lot of blood. He assured us that you would recover quickly with this." Lee pointed at the hanging bag.

"Where is Vick?"

Lee opened his mouth to speak but was interrupted when the door opened and a familiar face walked in. My eyes widened with excitement and I could feel a knot rise in my throat.

"Thia?" Tears filled my eyes.

She hurried to me and fell onto my chest and tightly held on to me. The tears couldn't be contained and I cried like an infant, soaking her hair and her neck as I held her close.

She pulled back ever so slightly and looked at me with a smile on her face and tears in her eyes.

"How did you get back?" I couldn't believe she was here.

"I'll tell you later; just rest up. We're going to need for you to be at your best before we do anything. We have some serious stuff to do and you're not going to like it, but you must trust me okay?"

I remembered what Gabriel said, that Thia should be trusted and that I should listen to her.

"I am just so happy to see you again!" I pulled her to me and held her tightly. I was afraid that if I loosened my grip she would disappear again.

"I love you so much." I cried as I held on to her.

"I love you too." Hearing her say those words to me began to heal every wound on my body.

"And I am going to be sick." Lee teased. I smiled and held up my middle finger for him.

I quickly cupped Thia's face in my hands and pulled her in for a kiss. This was a more passionate kiss than we had ever shared. A kiss that felt as if we were running out of time to be together and needed to enjoy each other as much as we could.

As her angelic lips enveloped mine, I began to think of our future and what Gabriel said about our love. Though forbidden, it was real and it was strong. And it wouldn't weaken under the stresses of this life. I knew that I had to do whatever possible to protect this love and Thia.

"Okay, I am seriously going to leave you two alone. Don't make any little vampire babies while I'm out." Lee stood up and headed to the door. I smiled as he turned to look at us one last time before walking out.

"Thanks Lee, for everything."

He nodded and walked out. I turned my attention back to Thia and just stared into her eyes. She was so incredibly beautiful. How had I not noticed this before? As I stared into her eyes, I could see this angel for what she truly was. Her eyes were bright and almost glowed as she smiled back at me. She was too good for this planet. Why the gods felt the need to damn such a beautiful and perfect being to this world was beyond me. She didn't belong here. She deserved to be in the heavens with the gods. I had begun to resent the gods and felt that they were even more wicked than the watchers.

For the first time, I began to empathize with the watchers and their ever growing hatred towards the humans. I understood their rage, resentment and, for a second, their desire to destroy the humans. The gods had given them everything, but it was never enough. The angels never asked for anything but served and loved the gods just the same. They felt rejected and cheated and that rage was fueling their desire to completely wipe out the humans. I wasn't even sure if I wanted to stop them anymore.

The gods would never accept me. I could walk straight up to the tree of life and I would still be damned for what my father did. There was no hope or redemption for my kind. So why was I trying so hard to help the humans and appease the gods? As I stared into Thia's eyes, it became clear to me. Even if I am never accepted or praised for doing good, I must still do it. It's what Thia believed in and what she had spent her entire earthly life trying to achieve. This was for her. Not the humans and certainly not the gods. It was for my dear Thia. At this point I didn't fear death unless it took me from Thia. I just wanted an end to all of this.

"Thia, when it's all over with, I want to ask you a very important question." I whispered to her softly as we continued to stare into each other's eyes.

"And what would that be?" She asked with a smile stretching across her face

"Well I can't ask now because it's not over with. But promise me that no matter what happens, that you will say yes, okay?" Her smile grew bigger as she began to piece together my words to discover what might be the question I hadn't yet asked.

"Well, that depends. If you are going to ask me to do your laundry, I will have to think about it. If you are going to ask me to fly ever again, I will most likely say no." She giggled as she leaned in to slowly kiss me, "But if you ask me to remain by your side for all of eternity, I can promise you that my answer will be yes."

As her words escaped her lips, so did the tears from my eyes. She wiped the tears from my face with her fingers and gave me a gentle kiss again.

Ruax was growing ever more anxious and angry as he paced around his dark and miserable cave. Two other figures approached him, their forms crooked and brittle in appearance. They were his personal slaves, whose only jobs were to gather information from the human world and report back to him.

"She arrived, master." One said in a low whisper-like growl.

"Good. She'd better not take too long or I will have to go rip out her insides."

Ruax huffed and continued to pace impatiently as the slave demons quickly left to avoid his wrath.

"You think you are clever, Thia. I can see right through you. Just know the penalty for deceiving me will be great." He growled as he watched Thia and Lafayette in his portal.

"So cuddly. I wonder what Azazel would say if he saw you loving on someone else."

He kicked the ground below him, spreading dust in a thick cloud around the chamber.

"This isn't over. I get what I want or all of mankind suffers.

With the blood IV, I was well on the mend. My head injury was not even a scar at this point and I felt life breathing back into me. As I lay in the bed for my last day, bored out of my head and flipping through my phone on my social media site, Thia sat beside me chuckling.

"What?"

"Social media. What do vampires share on social media?"

"I don't know. What does everyone else share? Cooking recipes? Pictures of cats? Ah, what about those who tell everyone everything about their lives. I can see it now, my latest status update, 'Man being a vampire can suck sometimes, pun intended. I got attacked by a demon and nearly ripped to shreds. I had to have a blood transfusion to help me survive. But I am a mean bastard so I bounced right back.' Ah look five hundred likes, six comments and a thumbs up?" I laughed.

"I think the modern touch on the life of vampires is a neat way to connect to people who have absolutely nothing in common with you." Thia rested her head on my shoulder.

"So what would a fallen angel's social media look like?"

She sat up slightly and cleared her throat.

"Well… 'Today I made a deal with a super bad-ass angel and he let me go on my word alone and I came back to see my boyfriend chewed up like a stick of gum'. Wait I should tag you in that." She giggled and gave me a playful punch to my side.

I looked at her with a questioning expression on my face.

"You made a deal with Ruax?"

Her smile instantly turned to a frown.

"I had to do something. He wasn't going to let me out of there alive if I hadn't."

"And what deal was that?"

She sighed heavily and stood up and walked to the door. She didn't look back as she began to explain.

"I told him I would get him the pendants so he could release Azazel."

I raised an eyebrow. "You did what?"

She turned to me. "I had to Lafayette. You don't know what it was like in that place. The constant screaming of tortured souls, his threats, the abuse he inflicted on me which I won't even get into. If I hadn't done what I did, he would have killed me. Then he would have come after you and the others. Bargaining the pendants was my only way to escape."

"What happens when you don't give him the pendants? No wait, I will answer that for you. He is going to kill us. Not just us but everyone associated with us. You, me, and Vick have a fighting chance. What about Lee and the others? They're humans. They aren't as strong as we are."

"I know that and I considered all of the repercussions when I made that deal. I figured once I was out of there we could all figure out what to do next."

"Did he say anything to you about a locket?"

She gave me a strange look. "What locket?"

"The old man that I obtained the second pendant from told me about a locket. All of the pendants fit inside of it and it becomes a master key of sorts. I really don't fully understand its purpose outside of that."

Thia grew very quiet as if she were thinking deeply about something. Her demeanor changed completely when I mentioned the locket.

"You know about this locket, don't you?" I suddenly realized that she and Vick had kept a lot of vital secrets from me and it was really starting to piss me off.

"I know about a locket. I never heard anything about the pendants relating to it. But only a few angels know about it. A long time ago, way before Earth was even created, the gods gave Lucifer a locket that held great power. It was only given to him because he was the most trusted and loyal angel. No one ever spoke of its purpose, not even Lucifer himself. When he was kicked out of Heaven he took the locket with him, but no one knew what ever came of it. Most of the watchers are not even aware that it still exists. There is one who knows about it though."

She walked back to me and sat beside me on the bed. "Azazel knows."

I sighed and slammed my fist onto the bed. "That's just great. The one that can rein complete chaos on this planet knows about something that can help him. Just great."

"If in fact the pendants have to all be combined in the locket, then we just need to make sure that the pendants and the locket never meet." Thia sounded so reassuring, but that wasn't the case for me.

"We need to separate these pendants. We need to hide them."

"What do you suggest?"

"I wish I knew. Maybe it's time to tell Vick and see what he suggests. He didn't seem to know anything about the locket when I told him earlier. Maybe with what you know it will help to jar his memory some. I have a feeling that he knows more than he's letting on."

Thia had a worried look on her face. *What was she not telling me?*

"Thia?"

She turned facing away from me and sighed.

"I have a long and complicated history with Azazel. We were once close, very close. You could say that we were in love. When we were cast out of Heaven, I never saw him again. I never knew what became of him, until recently. I harbor a lot of hated and resentment towards him now that I know he was here on this earth walking freely until the gods bound him deep inside of a mountain somewhere"

"You and Azazel were... lovers?" I was grimacing at the thought.

"Something like that. We could never consummate it because that was forbidden. I remained faithful, but it's obvious that he didn't. Once on Earth he unleashed his hatred and fury on the humans by mixing his blood with theirs and spitefully creating creatures like you. That's why he was cursed to that mountain. I feel that he did all of this because of me. If he is ever loosed and realizes what I have done by betraying the watchers, he will unleash his fury on me as well. This world will not be safe until he is damned to the deepest realm of Hell that exists."

"We won't let him escape. We have the pendants. Well, two of them. Not Ruax, not Azazel. As we search for the others, I promise you that nothing will happen to them once they are all in my hand. Then we will find the locket and bury his ass as far away from the tree of life as we can."

She smiled. "You are so confident. A little cocky, but hey, whatever works."

"Everything I do from here on out, is for you. Not for these vermin humans, not for the gods… but you alone. Without you here, I felt I had no purpose. I didn't feel alive anymore. To think I started out really hating you." I giggled and in turn she let out a cute, soft laugh.

"Well I didn't much like you either. You acted so stuffed up and uncaring. I have seen another side of you, a side that I couldn't resist; a side that I love. Our love is the most damned of them all. Angels just do not mix with vampires. So don't expect a lot of praise and congratulations from anyone outside of humans."

"Damn them all. This is our lives, Thia. This is our world and we have to live here like everyone else. Who cares what they think? I don't. I am going to get those pendants, restore humanity, and live happily ever after with my queen!"

She smiled and lay her head to my chest. "I hear your heart beating, Lafayette."

"It beats for you, my love."

CHAPTER TEN
Chaos

Things had certainly turned strange fast with the pendants in hand. I felt more empowered than before, but also more at risk of being discovered by the wrong beings. Lee and the others were consistently hacking into government sites all over the world trying to uncover their secret plans and so far all we knew was that they specifically kept a record of all the portals. Something felt out of place. It was as if evil was breathing down on us all and we couldn't pin point its exact location or what it would do next.

As we all sat around, bored out of our heads. Lee and his crew worked diligently trying to figure out the web sites they were hacking. I admired their ability to get into such heavily guarded sites. I didn't ask where they had acquired such knowledge. It was probably best that I didn't know.

"Hey, um, does anyone know what this might mean?" Asa peered up from his laptop screen. I quickly moved to him and focused on the screen in front of me.

"It looks like a blood type data base." I observed the chart on the screen.

"What would they want with a blood type data base?" Lee asked.

"It lists certain blood groups and has stars beside certain ones. Like type O+. I am not sure what this means, but do you think they are grouping the entire world based on their blood type?"

"If that's the case, we need to figure out why. Could it be a planned assault?" Asa asked.

"I think we need to keep an eye on this until we know for

sure." I continued to stare at the screen.

"Certain blood types are very popular while others are very rare. Then there are the negative ones. It's said that those are the blood traits of the angels that came here and bred with humans," Thia interjected.

"Ah well I am AB-, no shock there I guess," I replied.

"Most angels or angel hybrids have this blood type. It's how we're incredibly different from the average human. Even though some humans also possess the negative blood factor, it isn't widely known how pure their blood is. The watchers have been trying for centuries to track down all of the negative blood types. The humans that carry this are of particular interest to them." Thia locked eyes with me.

"And why is that?" Lee asked.

"Well, my guess is that they're humans with the blood line of the angels. Perhaps those are the ones they seek to help them obtain access to the tree of life."

"Why would the government be tagging those with positive blood?" Heratio asked.

"To eliminate them?" I shrugged my shoulders. It was just a guess, but I could be right.

"That's scary. I read an article once that stated each blood group reacts to diseases differently. Some blood groups are completely immune while others seem to be susceptible." Lee shivered as he spoke.

"So if the elites, under the guide of the watchers, were to create diseases to specifically target certain blood groups, the death toll could be catastrophic." Asa sighed deeply.

"I think they have already begun doing such." Thia put her hand on Asa's shoulder, "Looking at the last fifty years or so, the medical field has had many breakthroughs in developing vaccines to kill off a lot of diseases, but it seems that people are sicker now more than ever. I believe that with everyone receiving the same types of vaccines, it's actually making the diseases more resistant. They're becoming immune to the vaccines and some are even mutating."

"I heard about something similar in my home state. A flu

vaccine was introduced and was very successful in treating that particular strand. Then out of nowhere this super flu emerged and hit at epidemic proportions," Lee said.

"I think in all of their good intentions to eradicate these diseases, they are actually enabling them to mutate and become stronger. And this makes the people very vulnerable, depending on their blood types." Thia replied sadly.

"Why would the government intentionally go along with such a disastrous plan?" Heratio asked.

"Maybe they aren't aware. They think they're doing good." Thia turned to Heratio.

"So, since the watchers are already unleashing the foulest demons on earth and planning to wipe out humans, we can safely assume that this is something they might possibly try to do." I stood and stretched.

"This is just one way they'll launch their attack on humanity. There are other ways that they will make this destruction great and devastating," Vick chimed in.

"And what would that be?" I asked.

"The pendants represent the four elements. If they plan an assault based on those, you can expect not only diseases, but extreme weather and other disasters related to the pendants. They want to use what the gods have given man and destroy them with it."

"I suppose this would be a bad time to bring up the global warming debate." Lee said with a chuckle.

"Global warming is a hoax man," Heratio groaned.

"Is it? I'm sure the dinosaurs thought so too."

"Come on! We aren't going to debate global warming, religion, or politics here. We need to stay focused." There was a rise in her voice.

"I was just joking. Man your girlfriend's so stiff," Lee teased. Thia just gave him a look as if daggers would fly from her eyes and stab him in the throat.

"I believe everyone here is on the right page, at least for the most part. So let's just try to figure out which method they will use next in their assault and try to stop it. Or slow it down at least." Vick tapped his fingers on top of the laptop screen.

"I don't know about you guys, but I'm bored of being cooped up inside." I said abruptly knowing full well that Vick would give me hell about it.

"Lafayette," Vick began.

"Yes I know. Dangerous world. Look, immortal being bored. I want to go out and play! Come on Vick. What good am I fighting against this shit if I never leave the confines of a boring room?"

"I honestly have no argument this time," Vick huffed.

"I want to go to the park or something and just get some fresh air. This room is starting to smell like B.O. When was the last time any of you showered?" They all began sniffing their arm pits. Their reactions told me that they realized they did smell a bit gross.

"And… you shower? Lafayette?" Asa asked.

"I smell prettier than all of you!" They really couldn't argue. Though a vampire, I had exceptional hygiene. The rest of them smelled like that they had just crawled out of the sewers.

"Well, I guess it wouldn't hurt to get out of this musty room for a bit. And I am aching for something else to eat besides fast food. I think I have gained twenty pounds since hooking up with all of you." It was the first time Vick had said anything remotely humorous.

"I would kill for a danish right now!" Thia blurted out in excitement.

"And I would just literally kill for a pint of blood, seriously." They all slowly turned to look at me, each with their own look of disgust.

"What? I *am* vampire you know."

"Sometimes, Lafayette, you can be so human and then you mention blood and totally kill my vibe," Lee smirked.

It was a beautiful day for a stroll in the park; overcast,

gloomy, and cold. Though it suited me well, the others weren't so appreciative. Thia especially did not like the cold. As we walked, me more cheerful than the others, I could hear her moaning and groaning while her teeth chattered hard against the bitter cold. The others were also not as amused as I was.

"Aw come on! It's gorgeous out today!" I held my hands in the air.

People looked at me like I had fallen and bumped my head and my friends looked like they were two seconds from voting to leave me.

"Asshole!" Thia stuttered under multiple chatters.

I stepped closer to her and hung my arm around her shoulder.

"Don't worry baby, I'll keep you warm." I smiled and winked. She gave me a swift jab to my ribs that sent me doubled over to my knees.

Ah my bitchy Thia was back.

"Ow! Why must you be so mean?" I cringed from the throbbing pain.

"I'm freezing to death out here and you act like it's the middle of summer and we are in an amusement park. This is miserable!" She whined. God I missed this side of her so bad.

"Look at it this way, I am more hidden this way."

There was a commotion about twenty yards in front of us. People were running, some were screaming, and I couldn't tell what was going on. We picked up the pace as we moved towards the direction of the chaos. There were people everywhere circling around something that I couldn't see until we got closer.

Three bodies lay on the ground motionless, their skin gray. People were frantically dialing emergency personnel and others were attempting CPR on the lifeless beings. One was a man in his mid-thirties. His head was turned in a very unnatural way and I could immediately tell he was not alive. His blood smelled stagnant and decaying. Beside him was a woman in her early thirties. She was also lifeless and gray. Next to her was a child around the age of ten. All three of them appeared to be out for an afternoon stroll, enjoying their time together when something deadly had struck.

"They were just walking. I saw them," ane bystander cried out.

"The little boy was playing with a ball and then they just collapsed." Said another.

I moved in closer to have a look and a smell. It was as if these people had been dead for days. They already reeked of decay and their skin was beginning to turn black in some areas. Their eyes were glazed and horrified, indicating that their last moments were spent in excruciating pain. I quickly pushed my friends back away from the crowd.

"Those people said they were just out doing normal things when they all of a sudden collapsed. Yet they appear to have been dead for days," I explained.

"How is that even possible?" Lee asked trying to get a better look.

"I've never seen anything like this. It's like something attacked them, killed them, and sped up the decaying process," Vick added.

By this time, medics began to flood the area and everyone was ordered to move way back. They were now treating it as a hazardous situation.

"Ladies and gentlemen, I need you to move way back. Anyone who has come in contact with the bodies needs to report to the hospital immediately for observation," one of the medics ordered.

People began to flee in a panic and police quickly roped off the area forbidding access to anyone else who wasn't police or medical personnel.

"What's going on here?" Heratio asked, somewhat panicked himself.

"I believe the attacks we talked about earlier have begun," Vick whispered.

While the rest of the bystanders quickly dispersed from the scene, I couldn't help but remain near to observe the way the medics and police treated the bodies. They were immediately stuffed inside of hazardous waste body bags and a crew began to remove them from the scene. Cops stood guard over the area, not allowing anyone else to get too close.

What is this mysterious illness that just attacks, kills, and decomposes bodies so quickly?

It troubled me to see such panic and chaos here. I wanted to remain at the scene and watch, but the others were in a hurry to get as far from this place as they could.

We all left and headed down the street to a local restaurant. Hopefully the news of the bodies hadn't spread that far. As we entered, I saw a television hanging on the wall. News anchors were already discussing the mysterious deaths. *Word travels quickly here!*

We took a seat in a nearby booth and my eyes remained fixed on the broadcast.

"Local authorities are not commenting on the condition of the bodies or what may have caused the death. But are urging residents and anyone within a two block radius report to your local medical facility to be checked out and evaluated..."

"I find it odd how quickly the police and medics responded. Even more odd is how quickly the press picked up on this." Thia stared at the television.

"It's almost as if they knew it would happen." Lee's eyes were wide as he watched the news report.

A woman cleared her throat next to us. A server had come to our table, but we were all too distracted to even notice.

"Odd isn't it. Have you ever heard of such?" The waitress asked while staring at the news anchor.

"Odd indeed," I said in a low tone.

"Could we all have a glass of water please?" Vick asked.

"Certainly. I will bring those over while you check out the menu." She headed toward the kitchen.

"What's also odd is having a server at any restaurant here," I said.

"Yeah that used to be uncommon. I wonder what changed," Asa remarked.

"It's called the Royal Work force," Heratio clarified, "Putting people to work doing shitty jobs that didn't exist a few years ago."

"Is that a joke or are you being serious?" I asked.

"Shit, I don't know. I just said that. I don't know what it is really."

"Police have confirmed several more deaths in what doctors are calling the strangest sickness to sweep across this country in decades. They still don't know what the cause of it is, whether or not it's air born and how many others will become infected. What they do know is that it's quickly spreading and they don't know how or why. So anyone that suddenly falls ill is urged to seek treatment immediately."

"So, show of hands, who is ready to say bye-bye to the UK?" Lee added half-jokingly.

"We can't leave, not now. I am sure that with this outbreak and officials sent into a panic, they will quarantine the nation and not let anyone in or out." Vick shrugged.

Everyone grumbled in disgust, particularly Thia who had just about enough of this country.

"Authorities with the British Parliament have confirmed one of the members of the Labour Party has been found dead inside of his home earlier this afternoon. It has not been confirmed if he was infected by the mysterious illness or not, but only stating that his death was mysterious in nature."

"Oh great. So the elites are going to start dropping like flies now, too?" I groaned.

"I guess I have some homework to do when we get back to the room." Heratio sighed.

"Yes. I want you to find out who that party member was and all ties that he may have had with the watchers." Vick nodded.

"And in international news, an earthquake has just rocked Los Angeles, measuring a devastating 7.3 on the Richter scale. Multiple casualties have already been confirmed with several thousand still unaccounted for."

"On second thought, avoiding a mysterious illness here doesn't seem like such a bad plan," Lee groaned.

These two events that we'd all just witnessed today were linked together. It would get much worse unless we figured out how to stop it. I could feel the pendants in my pocket vibrating again. This time they felt angry, like they knew something bad was coming and was trying to warn me. I didn't alert the others about it. I knew it would just bring about more chaos and fear among the group. For now I just tried to ignore it as best as I could.

After our meal, we quickly made our way back to our room. The sun was starting to set and I knew that the creatures of the night would be emerging from their slumbers to do whatever the rest of them did. For me, I was always confined indoors at night, not allowed to freely roam about. It's as if Vick didn't trust me. I wasn't that tempted to feed on anyone here. I just enjoyed the chase. Vick was beginning to take all the fun out of being a vampire. I just wanted to go back and crash with Thia giving me a foot massage or something like that. I knew it would never happen, but I envisioned it nonetheless.

Since our old hotel room was growing way too small to accommodate everyone, we upgraded to a suite. I was relieved that at least now I could escape to a private room away from the others when they started to get on my nerves, which was most of the time. Especially Asa; I wasn't sure what bugged me most about him. Was it his competitive good looks, his cockiness, or the fact that he spent way too much time on the computer? I had always believed Heratio was the computer geek. And while he was very good at what he did, Asa seemed to be just a little better.

As the others went about their normal night time activities of hacking web sites, Thia and I retired to our master bedroom. We were not quick enough before Lee could crack off one final joke towards us.

"Hey Lafayette, do vampire babies breast feed?"

I turned and looked at him. "Really Lee? Why does your brain even think of things like that?"

"Well I don't know I was just thinking if you knocked up Thia would she do breast or bottle?"

Thia turned to him and replied almost instantly, "I do believe at this point, I would drain your neck and bottle feed the little vamp. Satisfied?"

Lee grinned. "Ah well in that case, be safe! We don't want any little vampire babies here now do we?"

"Good night Lee. Try not to overwork that pathetic chunk of gray matter you call a brain, okay?" I walked into the room and closed the door.

"So how *do* vampire babies eat?" I sounded almost as silly as Lee when I asked the question.

"Honestly Lafayette, you have been hanging around those idiots too long."

"It's a sensible question."

She huffed, somewhat annoyed, "They nurse like any other baby would. They don't develop strong vampire urges until their milk teeth come in; so it would be wise to wean the lil' blood sucker before that happens."

I smiled and pulled her close to me, staring into her eyes. "Lee has always poked fun at me for being a vampire. He's harmless though. Don't let him get to you."

"I just feel that right now, with all that's going on, there are too many jokes going around. It's like no one takes this mission seriously but me and you, and occasionally, Vick. Why are they even here, Lafayette?"

"Because I don't know a thing about computers and they do. I still haven't figured out how to change my mobile ring tone and that default ring is starting to piss me off. They can get into their systems and keep us just one more step ahead in case something really bad goes down. They will be able to warn us of anything before it happens. I know they get on your nerves. Just try to suck it up for a little while longer. When they aren't needed anymore they can go home."

She sighed and pressed her forehead to my chest.

"I don't know how much more of this place I can stand. I am seriously starting to reconsider my impression of the Hell Ruax had me in. Compared to this, it was paradise."

I lifted her chin for her to face me and smiled weakly.

"I know, but we have to remain here and keep searching for the portals, the dim wits that are following orders to destroy us, and hope that we don't screw this up."

She pulled away from me and walked to the bed where she fell backwards onto the firm mattress and sighed in a frustrated tone. I walked to her and slowly lay beside her, putting an arm across her chest.

"If we come out of this alive, I want a long vacation." She moaned.

"Sure. Where do you want to go"

"Somewhere warm and sunny."

"Well you do realize that might not work; vampire and all."

She shot me a grumpy expression and elbowed my side.

"Damn it woman. Stop jabbing me in the same place. I'm going to be forever bruised."

"I mean *after* all of this is over and we are both given human bodies and souls. Then the sun light won't affect you."

"Oh... right. Of course. I knew that."

"Sometimes I wonder if you have a brain in that skull of yours at all. Are you sure you and Lee aren't related?"

I gasped and my mouth dropped open.

"I'm deeply offended that you would even suggest such a thing!" I said. She grinned and pulled me to her for another kiss. One that began sweet and innocent and before long, I realized that we were heading down a road that neither of us should have ever considered.

As my clothes hung on a nearby chair, the pendants inside began to glow brightly. I was too busy to pay them much attention.

My dreams had become more vivid lately and far more terrifying. Now that Thia was back at least I wasn't waking from nightmares about her death, but so many things troubled me now that at times it had become difficult to discern dreams from reality.

The world was sick and slowly dying. Humans walked about as if they didn't notice or even care. Now they had begun to drop like flies, warning of the worst that was yet to come.

The tree of life had started to become a regular occurrence in my dreams, as well as the pendants and the locket that I had never physically seen.

It was night time in my dream and the moon shone brightly overhead drowning out any of the stars that were normally visible. I stood once again beside the old willow-like tree pondering everything that others had described to me. I could never be a part of this world no matter how hard I tried. I would never be able to taste the fruit of knowledge and be granted everlasting life outside of this cruel world. I began to wonder what exactly would happen to me once I was physically dead. No one had ever really explained that to me.

As I stood with my hand resting on the bark of the tree, the pendants vibrated in my pocket. I took each one out, holding them all in my hand by their chains. I held all four of them in my dream. The willow appeared thrilled to be near the pendants and long drooping leaves stretched out and caressed my hand in which I held them.

Out of nowhere, I was surrounded by a great darkness. One that was blacker than the night itself. Demonic beings encircled me, growling and gnashing their angry teeth. I stood still and tried to hide my fear. They snarled and repeatedly chanted my name in a voice that I can only describe as low, painful, and fierce. They began to move swiftly around me, their words striking out with every ounce of resentment they harbored. Although they hadn't physically assaulted me, their words felt like daggers to my heart. I tried to remain standing, but the force of their evil threw me to the ground where I lay in something warm and sticky. I immediately recognized the coppery smell. It was blood.

I raised my head and the entire scenery had changed. Now in my midst was a city completely engulfed in flames. Bodies were strewn everywhere and the streets were filled with cries and screams from people tortured, but not yet dead.

As I crawled along the ground trying to find my courage and strength to rise up and face this evil head on, I began to see familiar faces around me. It was my friends and they were all dead. Their blank eyes stared in such a way that told of the horrors they faced before their deaths. My eyes filled with tears and I began to call out to each one of them in a low whisper.

I continued to crawl slowly, my nails digging deep into the bloodied ground and, one by one, I passed by everyone that I had ever knew and loved. When I found Thia my mind went numb. Her body was mangled almost beyond recognition; her eyes wide and full of terror. Her shirt had been ripped open, exposing her chest cavity. Her heart was gone.

I began to panic and struggled to crawl towards her. Something grabbed my feet. I looked back and saw a figure that I didn't recognize. He was badly wounded and covered in blood. I tried to kick him off of me, but he clung on desperately.

He began to speak in a tired and defeated voice. "Azazel is loosed. Humanity is doomed. We are all doomed."

Frantically I struggled, kicking at him until he finally succumbed to his injuries and fell in a lifeless slump on the ground. I turned to face the burning city and saw the demons attacking mercilessly. People ran in all directions screaming and trying to elude this darkness that had ascended over them.

I watched as humans were struck down, one by one, by demons. Men, women, and even children lay in heaps with their blood quickly rising to form a river. No matter where I crawled, I was ankle deep in human blood. There seemed to be no end to this madness and misery. There was so much pain; so much death. I was supposed to save them but had failed.

A bright flash of light blinded me and, when it faded, I found myself in a sunny and magnificent garden. I could feel the presence of something good and pure, like an embodiment of perfection and beauty.

I was still on all fours and when I looked up, my eyes beheld the most wondrous being I ever saw standing over me. He extended his hand to me and with a kind gesture motioned for me to take it. Reluctantly, I obliged and was pulled up alongside of him.

"What you have seen has not yet happened. It is a vision of what could be if you fail this task, Lafayette."

"Who... what?"

"I am Uriel, you may have heard of me."

"Yeah. I've heard of you. I've heard of a lot of you. Archangels, right? So why have you allowed this great tragedy to take place? Why didn't you do as you were supposed to and protect mankind?" I realized my tone was abrasive and unforgiving.

"It was not the duty of angels to hold the hands of humans and never allow them to fall. They were created with free will and they do with that what they please. Some chose the righteous paths. Others followed the paths of greed, lust, and vengeance. We couldn't even stop some of the angels from going down that path. It's greed and lust that has caused all of this, not we archangels!"

"What can you tell me about Azazel? And this filthy creature called Ruax."

Uriel lowered his head and sighed. "When the sons of God fall, they fall worse than humans. With humans there is redemption and forgiveness. Angels will never be redeemed or forgiven. Azazel and Ruax were once beautiful and loyal heavenly beings whose only desires were to serve the gods that gave them life. Their jealousy was provoked by the creation of humans. They could not harness their anger and resentment towards the gods. It is unfortunate that you were thrown in the middle of all this. Even in all of your sins and wrong doings, you have remained a good being."

"Good? I feed off the blood of humans. How could there be anything good in me?"

"That is your nature. Just as it is the nature of a lion to slaughter a lamb, you can't help what you were created to be. Deep down you know that you do not deserve this fate. I agree with that, you don't."

Uriel stared intently into my eyes for what seemed like an eternity. I could not find any words that expressed my feelings of gratitude. He nodded, as if he understood my unspoken thoughts.

"Centuries back, prophecies told of a creature of the night rising out of the ashes of desolation and defeating the evil that had ensnared and enslaved humanity since the beginning of time. Only that which has the blood of Enoch would be able to do this. Enoch's bloodline was meant to remain pure and untouched by angels. That was not the case. Even though your bloodline is tainted by this abomination, you are still the last remaining carrier of this blood. The mission falls to you and you alone."

"What if I don't want this? What if I would rather just let mankind become extinct and the angels that caused all of this just fight each other to the death?"

"I don't think you want that. Not at all. You dream of becoming human and loving Thia for the rest of your lives. If you do this, I will personally make sure you get exactly just that."

"You know, everyone that I have encountered has told me the same thing, but they aren't telling me something important! How do I defeat the watchers?"

Uriel turned to a rose bush beside him and plucked one of the blooms from it.

"A rose is known for its incredible beauty and sweet scent. Many seek them and wish to obtain these magnificent flowers. They forget about the ugly side of a rose. It's sharp and unforgiving thorns. In order to grasp the rose in your hands, you have to carefully weave through the chaos of thorns and oftentimes, the seekers are pricked by these. However, the satisfaction of holding a rose in one's hand defeats any of the anguish they may have encountered to obtain it."

Uriel handed me the rose and a single thorn pricked my finger tip. I flinched and held my bleeding finger to my lips.

"In order for you to gain the beauty of eternal life here in Heaven, you will have to weave through the ugly and bitterly painful side of Hell. One by one, you will have to pluck away the thorns that stand in your way."

The angel smiled sadly at me. He knew. He knew what he was asking me to do was nearly impossible.

"For now, Azazel remains locked inside of his prison. Only you hold the keys to unleashing him. This power is yours and yours alone. You can use this power to destroy evil or you can use it to become a more powerful creature than anything in all of the heavens or hells. Your immortal side may be tempted to take the latter, but it's your human side that will prevail. Once you have defeated this darkness, the keys will lead you to the tree of life where you will have all that I have promised ."

"Ruax is too strong for me. And Azazel will be too. I can't defeat them, not alone."

"Without all of the pendants you won't be able to. That is why you have to find them before Ruax does. Once all of these stones are in your hands, you will be able to defeat them. I warn you, each stone you obtain will also bring destruction to the land. Each time a pendant is discovered, it will become a beacon to the watchers so you won't be able to stay hidden once you have them."

"I haven't exactly been able to hide too well from them as it is. No matter where I go or what I do, they always find us."

"Thia is a watcher, Lafayette. What you did tonight comes with great consequences."

I thought for a moment and then it hit me. *Oh shit!*

"You have done what cannot be undone and the penalty for your actions will be great. The physical unity between angel and vampire has been banned for a reason. You know of that which I speak."

I felt really awkward and embarrassed that we were even having this discussion. I was not about to pour out my heart to this angel and try to convince him that I was right in my actions simply because I love her.

"But we can't dwell on that for now. It's not as important as what is to come. The riders of the four horses have already begun to unleash their destruction over the earth. Wherever you look there is war, sickness, famine, and ultimately death will consume mankind. You saw it earlier today. That is only a taste of what is coming."

"This has been going on for thousands of years. What makes it so special now?"

Uriel cleared his throat and put his hand on my shoulder.

"Because the chess pieces are in place now, for centuries they have been lining up the board in preparation for their attack. It is almost time. Go, the pendants await you. Hurry and find them. Keep them safe and restore mankind to their beauty and glory."

As I raised my head to look at him, I found myself sitting upright in my bed looking around the room. It was morning and the sun was beaming through the window. I looked at Thia, who lay under the blanket sleeping soundly.

As I stirred in the bed, she slowly opened her eyes and looked at me with a smile on her face. Her smile quickly faded and she bore a look of panic on her face.

"Oh my god! Lafayette, what did we do?" She sat up quickly, pulling the blanket tightly around her.

"Yeah, believe me, I have already been scolded by Uriel so please don't remind me."

"Uriel? You spoke to Uriel? How?"

"Well, in a dream, I think. It seemed so real though. He said that our actions would come with serious consequences."

"I can't believe we were so careless! Oh my God Lafayette, this is bad!"

I leaned toward her, propping on one elbow and slowly moved a strand of hair that was covering her eyes.

"Whatever is thrown at us, we will defeat it. I regret nothing about last night and you shouldn't either."

"I'm scared, Lafayette." Her lips quivered slightly and I put my hand to her cheek.

"Me too, my love. Me too."

CHAPTER ELEVEN
The Countdown Begins

Every news outlet around the world was now broadcasting the sudden and mysterious deaths in England. The disease, whatever it was, had begun to spread to other parts of the globe. England was now shut down to anyone coming in or out. It was martial law in a sense. A curfew was established and anyone caught outside after 9 p.m. were immediately arrested. As the death toll climbed into the thousands, health officials scrambled to understand what was going on.

Being on such a short leash would make things more difficult for us now. The other pendants were out there somewhere and I had to find them. So little time to do it during the evening meant that we would have to do so in broad daylight, which wouldn't be an issue if the sun remained hidden by clouds. Lately, this seemed to change as well. England was experiencing more sunny days than usual and on those days I had to hide inside of the hotel. Lee and the others would have to venture out for me on those days.

No one suspected anything out of the norm with Thia and me at first. Soon, we began to show signs that something wasn't right. We seemed very rigid and uncomfortable around each other which alerted the others that something was amiss.

Lee, Heratio and Asa were preparing to head out and do some "field work," as they liked to call it and I was trying to distract my bored mind by watching TV. Thia was on her phone as usual.

"God the TV here sucks. I'm seriously about to stream some movies or something." I threw the remote to the TV down on the couch.

"Let's hope they get to the bottom of these deaths soon and lift the curfew. Then you can go out at night more." Lee tried to soothe me as he put on his coat.

"I'm bored out of my head. I'm also hungry. Vick, you might need to make another run to your doctor friend."

"Well there is a problem with that, too, Lafayette." Vick spoke slowly.

I looked up at him as he continued, "With all of these deaths and no one knowing what is causing it, any and all blood stored in the vaults are being carefully guarded. Not even the doctor himself can gain access to them now. If this is a blood born disease, you could be affected too."

"So am I supposed to just sit here and do nothing while I starve to death?"

"I don't know what to do. My hands are tied."

I huffed in frustration and stood up and walked to the window.

"I can't stand it here anymore. I want to go home." It was obvious everyone in the room felt the same, but we were powerless to do anything about it for the time being.

"Just try to hang in there man." Lee consoled. It wasn't much comfort since he could eat anything he desired. I felt as if I were slowly withering away.

Thia was very quiet during all of this which made everyone suspicious.

"What about you, Thia?" Lee gently coaxed.

She slowly looked up from her phone, looking towards me then at Lee.

"What about me?" She asked in a rather panic tone.

"Do you want something to eat? Something sweet maybe?"

"Oh, right. Yeah anything sweet. An angel's got to eat you know."

"So do vampires," I mumbled.

"You want me to slaughter something for you and bring back some blood, right?" Lee rolled his eyes, sounding almost condescending.

"No. Like Vick said, if that person is sick, I could be affected.

I will just pretend I am fasting."

"Who said it had to be a human? There are tons of wharf rats around here."

I turned to face him.

"That's just nasty man. I am nowhere near that hungry yet."

"Well okay. How about a nice bloody steak?"

I grimaced at the thought. I was so sick of steaks. The blood was satisfying but the flesh made me feel ill.

"Yeah get me one on the rare side. In fact, just go to the store and pick me up a raw one. I guess I could suck on it like a lollipop or something."

Lee's face scrunched up in disgust.

"And you think the rat idea was gross? I'll get you one."

"You guys be careful. The watchers know that you are affiliated with us. There is no telling what they will do next." Vick warned.

"According to what we have uncovered on the websites, it seems right now they are just hell bent on mass murder. And, well, trying to find the location of the pendants. I don't think they are really watching us at the moment, but we'll be careful." Asa said as he put on his coat.

"We will be careful," Lee assured Vick.

With that, they each walked out of the door leaving behind me, Thia, and Vick.

That's when Vick turned his attention to me and Thia.

"And what is with you two? You have been acting very awkward lately."

Thia looked at me, rather shocked by his questioning and I mentally searched for a satisfying excuse.

"We're just tired of being here. There's so much to do, but yet we're prisoners in this place."

"We are all feeling like that. But you two… what is going on?"

Thia sighed and looked at me.

"Just tell him, Lafayette. We won't be able to hide this forever."

"Hide what?" he asked, looking at me.

I was flustered. I didn't want to have to tell Vick such a personal thing, but Thia was right; this was something that could have consequences that we wouldn't be able to hide and we needed to know how to prepare for it.

"Okay. Don't start yelling at me or I will take out my hunger on you?"

Vick nodded.

"You know that one thing we vampires were forbidden to do, especially with other angels?"

By now Vick had caught on and did not look pleased at all.

"Please tell me you didn't!" He scolded.

"We did —," Thia started.

"Do you two understand why vampires were ordered not to do that?"

"Yeah, but come on. There are vampires everywhere doing the same thing. I really don't think we alone should be condemned for it."

"Lafayette, your blood is special. So special that it should not ever mingle with another creature like that, human, demon, or angel. What if Thia becomes pregnant? Do you understand what that creature will be like?"

"I have already had this discussion with Uriel. I know full well what could happen. It's too late to ponder that now."

"How did you talk to Uriel?" Vick seemed confused at this point.

"In a dream." I turned back to the window and spoke, "He told me about a prophecy regarding me and the pendants. Right now, the most important thing is to get those pendants. Whatever else happens we'll deal with when we have to."

"You are so reckless and inconsiderate, didn't you know?" Vick's tone was angry now and I just didn't want to deal with his criticism.

"I'm part human, you know. You and the order and everyone else has propped me up as being this amazing immortal being. You forget I have a human side that I also can't ignore. Don't sit there and try to tell me what I am doing wrong when you have not once in your life had to live your life as half human and half immortal." I raised my voice, growing even more frustrated.

"Vick, we know that what we did was probably careless and selfish. We also knew that our feelings for each other couldn't be harnessed any longer. Please don't be angry with us." Thia's voice was gentle but firm.

Vick sighed.

"I don't know what I am going to do with you two. There is a war going on out there and you actually take your minds off the mission to focus on other things."

"We have never taken our minds off the mission!" I blurted out. "That is all that we have thought about since coming here. The order tricked us, they lied to us. They sent us here to destroy the very ones they are using to try to kill us. We have to find some stupid pendants and destroy a super pissed angel hidden in the ground somewhere and for once we get away mentally so that we don't shut completely down and you want to drill us about being reckless?" I sat back down on the couch and flipped through the TV.

"Look at this shit. Everywhere we turn is bad news. People dying; governments becoming more powerful and more blood thirsty. I cannot physically cope with this every second of the day and especially without proper nourishment. So take your opinions and shove them up your ass. I'm done trying to be the perfect immortal for you Vick."

Vick sighed and walked to the door.

"I don't know whose side you are on anymore, Lafayette. I am not even sure you are the man for the job. But what I do know is that someone has to stop this. If you can't do it, then you need to let me know."

"I need you to get off my ass for five minutes and let me try to figure this out." I said without looking at him.

"Fine, I will leave you two to 'discuss' the mission and decide what you want to do." He reached for the door handle and Thia stood up.

"Where are you going?" She asked.

"I don't know anymore." Then he walked out and slammed the door.

I looked at Thia who seemed just as confused as I was about Vick's outbursts.

"I hate to say it, but I think we are about to be alone in this mission."

"I hate to say it, but I think you're right."

Lee, Asa, and Heratio ventured out into the city not really knowing where they were going or what to do. Lucky for them they were humans and not confined because of sun light. All they had to worry about was some mysterious disease.

"Did Vick seem a little tense to you?" Asa asked as they walked down the side walk.

"More so than usual. Particularly at Lafayette and Thia. I wonder what's going on there." Lee added.

"I think he feels what I have felt for a while but didn't think it was my place to say anything."

"And what is that?"

"That Lafayette is too distracted by Thia to complete this mission. How much time did we spend when we first arrived here, looking for her and trying to figure out how to get her back, instead of how to find and take out these evil watchers?"

"Hmm. You're right, but what can anyone do? That's the love of his life. We can't interfere with that." Lee's voice dropped low.

"I didn't get drug all the way to this place to just sit in a hotel room playing cards and waiting on someone to decide what the hell to do. I think it's time we took matters into our own hands." Asa whispered.

Lee stopped and looked at him.

"What are you saying?"

"That maybe we should leave the group and try to sort this out ourselves. We already have the knowledge to get inside of the governments most secret files and decipher what is going on. What do we need those three for?"

"It's not that we need them. They need us," Lee added as he

began to walk again.

"They are holding us back. If we go out there and find these watchers on our own and destroy them, we'll be the heroes."

"I don't want to be a hero. I'm only here to help my friend. If you two want to abandon them, that's fine. You go right ahead, but my loyalty is to him and I'm not going anywhere."

"Well I want this all to end so we can get back home. I have a woman there who needs me too." Asa interjected.

"You two do what you think you have to do. I'm not going anywhere until we all finish this."

"And what if your friend can't do this?" Asa asked.

Lee stared at him, "A captain goes down with the ship. Friends don't abandon each other when things get rough. I have faith that he'll do this. He was born for this. You don't know him like I do."

"You're right. We don't know him. For all we know he could go a little insane from hunger and kill us all. Or he could become so distracted by his little bitch that he puts us all at risk."

Lee turned to Asa, grabbed him by his shirt collar, and pushed him against a nearby wall.

"Don't you *ever* say anything bad about him or Thia ever again, Got it?"

"Or what Lee? Are you going to get your vampire friend to save you like you always have?"

Lee realized that what he said was partially true. He threw his hands down at his side and looked at them both.

"We're done here." Lee turned in the opposite direction and began to walk away.

Heratio started to go after him, but Asa grabbed his arm.

"Just let him go man. Let them all go. Let's try to figure out what to do."

"You do realize we have no cash, right? They brought us here, they have the bank cards and we have nothing."

"Oh I never go anywhere unprepared." Asa smiled and reached into his pocket and pulled out a credit card.

Heratio looked at the card and then at Asa.

"So what do you suggest we do now?"

"I think it's time to go sightseeing. I think we should start with that gorgeous clock tower. Who knows, maybe we will run into some bad guys along the way."

"And then do what? We don't even know how to recognize the watchers if we were face to face with them."

"You may not, but I do." Asa grinned devilishly.

Sometime later the hotel door flung wide open, sending all three of us into instant attack mode. We realized it was just Lee and, though relieved, we were a bit curious where the others were.

"Lee, what's going on? Where are the others?" I could tell he was upset.

"They wanted to be dicks and act like they can do this on their own so I left them." Lee sat down on the couch beside me.

"Do what on their own?" Thia asked.

"I don't know, man. They think that because they're computer geeks that they know more than any of us. I just got sick of listening to them. If they come back, great; if not, whatever, but I won't let them dog my friends down like they did and pretend to be friends with them."

"Dog us down? What did they say?" I asked, now even more curious as to what happened.

"Forget it, man. It's not important. All it will do is piss you off more. I'm just going to sit here with you guys until we decide what to do."

"We don't know what to do," Thia said.

"I think it's time to use those pendants, Lafayette." Vick came through the door.

I looked at him. His eyes were narrow and he chewed on his bottom lip. *How did he pop up so suddenly?*

"Use them for what?"

"Use them to draw out the watchers and just start eliminating them one by one."

"Well that sounds like a whole lot of hell no!" Thia objected.

"Which is why we should do it. We have run out of options otherwise. I'm sick of being here. I want to be doing something. Even if it's dangerous it's better than dying of boredom." I held Thia's arm gently as I spoke.

"Let me see the pendants." Vick held out his hand.

I reached into my pocket and took them out and handed them to him.

"These pendants are not very powerful individually. The more we combine together, the more powerful they become; especially in your hands, Lafayette. The watchers are seeking them and if you use their power, they will find us."

"Great. That sounds like fun. Can I eat first? I won't be powerful enough on an empty stomach."

Vick sighed and shook his head.

"I really hate to do this. To suggest it is even more insane, but desperate times calls for desperate measures." Vick stood.

I looked at Thia and she shrugged.

"Desperate for what?" I asked.

Vick walked toward me, unbuttoning his shirt.

"You can't kill me. Weaken me, perhaps. But I will live."

"Oh hell no! You aren't suggesting I —."

"I am. It is the only option we have. If you are too weak, we will all lose. With my blood, you will become even stronger for longer periods."

"This is really awkward." Lee stared wide-eyed at the scene unfolding in front of him.

"Tell me about it," I agreed.

"This is also forbidden. Due to the circumstances, I don't feel that we have a choice. Like you said earlier, we will face the consequences later. For now, we have to survive. Be warned, the blood that I carry is angelic blood and very potent. You may find it difficult to stop once you have started. Only take what you need and control your lust for more."

"What if I can't stop? It has been so long since I drank fresh blood. I don't know how to control myself."

Vick leaned over, handing the pendants to Thia.

"You will control him with these. If he has had his fill but doesn't want to let go, use the pendants."

"How?" she asked looking at the pendants.

"It's kind of like a gun. Just point and shoot. The pendants will do the rest. They will react to your desires and will."

"I've never used a gun either. Let's hope my aim isn't off." She sounded a bit apprehensive.

I turned to her and took her hand in mine. Then I nodded confidently.

Vick sat beside me and moved his shirt out from around his neck.

Lee almost seemed nervous about what was going to take place. I was nervous as well, but tried to look courageous.

I looked at his neck, thick veins pulsing and inviting me to feast on them. I could feel my fangs extending, something I hadn't experienced in a long time, and slowly I moved in placing my mouth to Vick's neck. I glanced up at Thia and Lee who were very nervous. Lee turned his back to us, not wanting to watch.

I heard Vick take a deep breath to prepare for the pain he was about to experience.

"Thank you for this Vick," I said as I pierced through his skin with my teeth.

His body went rigid as he tried not to fight me. My mouth filled with the strongest blood I had ever come in contact with. I wondered why I hadn't feasted on an angel before. Vick struggled to cover his mouth to muffle any sounds coming out. As his blood entered into my body I immediately felt much stronger. The taste was so good that I indeed wanted more.

I couldn't stop myself. Even after I'd had my fill, I just wanted more and more. Vick began to slap against my arm that held on to him in sort of a head lock. I ignored him. I tried to stop, but something inside of me wouldn't let me. Lee noticed and ran to me and tried to pry me off. I held up my hand and shoved him back against the wall. He landed with a thud and struggled to regain his senses.

Vick desperately reached for Thia who held the pendants in her hands. She froze with fear as Vick pleaded with her with his hands for her to stop me.

She shook her head, held up the pendants towards me, and that's when it was like an explosion took place. I was sent flying across the room, away from Vick and landing not far from Lee.

I began to return to my senses and realized what had just taken place. All at once, I could feel the power of Vick's blood and the power of the pendants. It was like a new high I had never experienced and I liked it.

"Whoa. That was amazing!" I smiled.

Thia held a cloth over Vick's neck as he sat up some, a little weak but alive.

"I warned you. And now you understand why you were ordered to never do that," Vick said in a weak raspy voice.

"Can I do that to the watchers?" I stood up feeling like a new man.

"That was literally the scariest thing I've ever seen." Lee hung his mouth wide open and a fear I had never seen before shown on his face.

"Yeah. Sorry about that buddy. Let's hope we don't have to do that again any time soon, at least not when you're around."

"When I regain my own strength, we will leave. We still have several hours until the curfew," Vick said rubbing his wound. Small droplets of blood dripped down on his shirt and my eyes grew wide with desire for more.

"Calm yourself, Lafayette. Don't make me use these again," Thia warned playfully, holding up the pendants.

I certainly wanted no more of that. I felt refreshed and more energized, I had a headache from hell now and I was sure the wall would never recover from that. I wondered if the neighboring people heard the commotion and how I would explain it if confronted. Somehow, we had always managed to go unnoticed by most. Folks didn't want to question why two young looking freaks, an old man, and three computer nerds were sharing a room.

土

Heratio and Asa arrived at the clock tower. Even though Heratio had no idea what they were doing, Asa seemed very certain.

"So what are we here for?" Heratio asked as they stood over the Westminster bridge, looking out over the river. The sun was partly shining through fading clouds and Asa's appearance seemed to change. Heratio didn't notice right off.

"Do you know how much evil gathers in that big old building there each day?" Asa asked.

"Probably everyone that goes in?" Heratio was puzzled by his question and wasn't sure how to answer.

"Everyone in there not only decides the fate for this country, but pretty much the entire world. That is a lot of power for one building to possess."

"I guess so." Heratio seemed bored of the topic and not really wanting to reply. Asa seemed aggressive in his plan to uncover the evil deeds taking place inside. He was not even concerned about being exposed or arrested. This was the sort of recklessness that Vick had wanted to avoid.

"Ah look, some of the freaks are emerging from their cave. Let's go!" Asa said.

Heratio looked to his right and saw a line of people exiting the door nearest them. He was filled with apprehension and uncertainty, but Asa was adamant about moving in closer.

"What are you doing?" Heratio asked as he trotted along behind Asa.

Asa said nothing. As they grew closer to the people, Heratio knew something was wrong. Asa changed in an instant. He turned into a monster right before his eyes. His nostrils flared, his shoulders went rigid, and his eyes almost seemed to glow a deep red color.

"Asa?!" Heratio called.

Asa continued to ignore him. They were fast approaching the line of people and Asa's steps grew quicker with each step he took. Finally, as he reached a few yards from the crowd, Heratio stopped; fearing the worst and not wanting to be any part of it. He could hear Asa shouting at them, though he couldn't make out exactly what he was saying. Before anyone had time to react, Asa dove on several men as the armed guards moved in to dismantle the attack.

Heratio's eyes widened and his mouth dropped open. He couldn't believe what he was seeing. There were screams and panic all around. Asa did not appear to be losing. He fought off five guards at once while he continued to savagely attack the Parliament people. Heratio saw something that he did not expect to ever see from his trusted friend. Asa donned the fangs of an animal and viciously ripped into the necks of several people including a guardsman that tried to intervene.

"Oh my God, Asa!" he whispered as he covered his mouth in fright.

The scene turned chaotic and deadly and the area around them filled with blood. He decided that it was time to get out of there, and fast! He took off running in the opposite direction of the massacre as he heard emergency sirens approaching. He was terrified that his friend would come after him next. How had he managed to hide such a dark secret for so long?

Back at the hotel, Vick was recovering from his wound when suddenly the door swung open and a terrified Heratio ran in.

"What on earth happened to you man? You look like you've seen a ghost." Lee jumped to his feet in concern.

Heratio bent forward, placing his hands on his knees trying to catch his breath.

"Turn on the TV. I'm sure it's all over the news by now," Heratio gasped.

I picked up the remote and flipped on the TV. Just as he said, something was going on.

"There was an attack on members of Parliament just moments ago

as a crazed man viciously assaulted everyone in the area, killing two and critically wounding several more including members of the Royal guard. Before police could apprehend the suspect, he fled on foot. An artist sketch depicts something not even human and more like an animal of sorts. Witnesses claim the creature was indeed human moments before the attack."

"Asa... he went crazy! I've never seen anything like that. He changed in a second to some sort of beast. I couldn't tell what exactly. Except that he was big and strong and had these large teeth extending from a very powerful maw."

"You brought a werewolf into our midst?" I asked turning my glare at Lee.

He looked just as shocked as the rest of us.

"How the hell could I possibly know about that?"

"You're his friend. How long have you known him?" I added in an unforgiving tone.

"We have been friends for about eight years. He's never shown this side of himself before, I promise. He was always interested in the occult and vampires, but I never gave it any thought. I mean seriously, who ISN'T obsessed with those things these days?"

"You brought a werewolf into our midst!" I repeated more aggressively.

"I'm sorry man. You know I wouldn't have done that on purpose."

"And when you told him you were traveling here to help a vampire, what did he say exactly?"

Lee thought for a moment then frowned.

"Come to think of it, he did seem overly enthused about it. I just assumed it was because he would be working alongside something he had read about in mythology that people have long since declared to be just stories. I didn't know! *Okay?*"

I sighed and rubbed my temples. I couldn't tell if it was the stress getting to me or the increase of power since feasting on Vick's blood.

"Why would he attack those people like that?" Thia was staring at the TV screen in shock.

"He said something about the evil there. Earlier he said you guys weren't doing enough to stop it. I guess he decided to take matters into his own hands." Heratio replied.

"Great, so you bring a creature here that you know hates my kind, even though you may not have known about his secret, he's here causing even more panic and chaos than there already is. Great!" I was frustrated and somewhat concerned. But at the same time, I was yelling at my friend who seemed to have been totally clueless about Asa.

"He was just a really good computer geek, man," Lee added with a deep sigh of regret.

"So if vampires and werewolves are enemies, why did he help us for so long? Why not attack you the many times he had a chance to?" Thia questioned, which added to the confusion.

"Maybe because there are much bigger issues than a vampire and werewolf squabble," Vick reiterated.

"Well whatever his intentions, he just made things way worse." I said blowing out my frustration in a large gulp of air.

"Perhaps that was the plan all along," Vick began. "With that sort of attack on the Royal members, those inside who are indeed under the eyes of the watchers would report the incident to them and they will know that someone is on to their plans."

Vick turned his gaze to Lee, "That guy you saw on the plane, how well was he watching you all?"

Lee thought for a moment, "He was watching us as if we were putting on a show for him, why?"

"Then he knows that Asa was with you and that you came here to meet up with Lafayette. Is it possible that Asa knew about the watchers prior to coming here? If so could he have been secretly working for them?"

This line of questioning seemed to upset both Heratio and Lee. None wanted to accept their friend as a traitor, let alone killer.

"He is our friend. He has been there for me through some pretty bad shit man. I can't believe he knew about any of this. And I don't believe he would betray us." Lee choked up, nearly in tears. It was obvious that this was a lot to take in for him and that he didn't want to believe any of it.

"We can't trust him anymore," Vick said as he lowered his head in condolences to Lee. "He attacked people without the permission of this group and he did so without any regards to our own safety. And he's obviously not completely human. What *is* he exactly is still the question to ask."

"Yeah and while we are at it, Lafayette, you're supposed to be able to recognize these things. You're constantly looking over your shoulder for anyone that is not completely human. How did you miss this?" Lee asked as he glared at me.

"I... I don't know. I guess it's because I've been looking for watchers, who are angels, and demons who were also once angels. I didn't notice because I wasn't looking. I always felt a strange vibe from him from the first day we met. It never occurred to me that he was anything but human. That's my error and one that I deeply regret now."

"He won't stop now. He is still out there, somewhere and I can only guess that there will be more attacks like this. But is he trying to help us? Or trying to snuff us out of hiding?" Vick looked around the group.

"We will have to be on extra guard from now on. Wherever we go, we have to be very mindful of our surroundings. The watchers will not stop now until they have eliminated any and all threats to their order. This includes any humans who we are associated with."

Vick turned to me, "It's time that we break up into two groups. They will be searching for you Lafayette, and you as well Thia. Maybe now Asa as well, depending on which side he's on. We can't trust him. From now on, he is our enemy and if we should happen upon him —."

Vick turned his gaze to Lee, who was still upset by the whole ordeal, "Kill him!"

CHAPTER TWELVE
Dawn of Evil

As I tried to lull myself to sleep that night with Thia clinging frightfully to me, I couldn't help but to feel a bit betrayed by Lee. Even though he really had no idea this would happen and that his friend was some sort of creature, he was responsible.

Either directly or indirectly, he brought him here. Now our plans had once again changed. We didn't know what we were up against, but we knew that it was about to get much worse.

As everyone lay sleeping, I tried to come up with a plan. I had nothing. The pendants I would need to collect to become powerful enough to face off against Azazel, the locket that existed and no one knew much about, that damned Ruax and his temper tantrums, mine and Thia's budding forbidden romance, and now Asa which plagued my deepest thoughts and for whatever reason made me feel more apprehensive than all of the other things combined.

We vampires and werewolves were not known as close friends, but in the short time that I had spent with Asa he didn't strike me as someone I needed to fear. He was clever, handsome, and seemed to harbor a lot of resentment towards angels; which had nothing to do with him at all. He almost had an unnatural curiosity in them and always wanted to know what their exact plans were and where they were located. Though he had proven to be a very valuable asset to the group, he had also now become a liability.

My thoughts were interrupted by a loud explosion outside of our hotel. I immediately sprung from the bed in fear as the others were jolted from their sleeps. In a panic we were all driven to the window to see what was going on. As we looked out, we could see a huge fireball extend high into the air. People were running and screaming and it still wasn't clear what had caused it. Before any of us had time to react, another explosion rocked the foundation of the hotel, sending each of us stumbling to the floor.

"What the hell is that?!" Lee screamed. I looked at Thia who appeared terrified.

I quickly jumped to my feet and peered back out of the window. Fire had engulfed the nearby buildings and it became clear to me that we would have to flee for our lives.

"We have to go!" I shouted to the others.

"Go where?!" Heratio cried out as he coughed from the smoke that was quickly bellowing through our hotel door.

"We have to hurry! Quickly, everyone follow me!" Vick commanded as he stumbled to the door, opening it wide. The entire area was pure chaos. People were running and screaming, some were obviously wounded and we still did not know what had caused the explosions.

As Vick held the door open, Lee, Thia and myself ran out. Heratio turned scampered toward the rear of the room.

"Heratio! Come on!" I yelled.

He returned with his laptop in hand, which I thought was a rather careless move considering the dangers we were now in. After everyone had exited the room, I led them all down the stairs leading to the parking lot. Another explosion hit and sent us all to the ground once more. This time we recovered much more quickly and darted off into the shadows of a nearby tree line. Once out of sight, we glanced back at the pandemonium unfolding. We heard sounds that had become far too familiar with us. The sounds of demons screeching.

I had to think quickly. The demons were fast approaching and I wasn't fully aware what we would be up against. We turned towards the thick trees and began to run. I was in front followed by Thia, then Vick, then Lee and Heratio.

I knew that we would not be able to outrun the demons and it was becoming clear that we might not escape this time. The entire area was on fire, there were multiple demons closing in on us and I was frantically trying to lead the group to safety.

Vick called out for me. I stopped and turned to him.

"Lafayette, use the pendants. Get everyone to safety!" He cried out.

Once again, I completely forgot about the pendants that were now violently vibrating in my pocket.

"What about you!?" I screamed.

"I will hold them off until I know you are all safe!"

I paused and realized what his true intent was. He could easily go with us, but they would still come after us. Even if we stayed in that little hidden box for a week, they would be there waiting on us when we emerged. They weren't going to stop this time. Vick would take them all on while we made our escape. I wasn't sure if the old man could defeat them. This was one time he was not going to run anymore. If he went down, he was taking them with him.

"Go Lafayette! Go!" he ordered.

I heard a loud scream and looked up into the sky to see these black winged creatures circling above us. They looped and began a nose dive in our direction.

I scrambled to retrieve the pendants from my pocket. I watched in horror as the creatures descended on Vick. He held out his hands towards them and a bright ball of energy like lightning shot out of his fingertips. The creatures were stunned briefly and then dove towards him again.

I pulled the pendants from my pocket, grabbed on to my friends, and in an instant we were gone.

As we slowly woke from being unconscious, we didn't find ourselves in a black room. We were in the middle of a very large room which had the appearance of a castle great hall. We slowly stood, looking around at this magnificent room and what we could only guess was beyond this place.

The floors were a dark gray marble polished so fine that it

looked like a glistening body of water. The walls were lighter gray marble bricks stacked one on the other and not as shiny as the floors. On the far end of the room was a very large fireplace, so big that each of us could stand inside of it with our arms outstretched and still not be able to reach from one side to the other. There were various old paintings on the walls that appeared to be the faces of angels, demons, Heaven, and Hell. It was an unsettling sight and I wondered how we had gotten here. There were old Victorian style couches, one on each side of the room, that appeared aged and worn and illuminating the creepiness of this place.

"Where are we, Lafayette?" Thia asked grasping my arm. I looked around, still puzzled myself.

"I have no idea." I was in awe as I tried to absorb the incredible beauty of this place.

We heard footsteps behind us, slowly moving in our direction with a loud clapping sound as shoes slammed against the marbled floors. Slowly we turned to face that which was closing in on us.

My mouth dropped wide open, as did the others as horror overcame us. Thia grabbed onto my hand tightly and I felt Lee push up against me from behind.

"You!" I cried out.

"Hello my friends. You're late!"

Asa stood before us with an evil grin on his face.

About the Author

Amanda Zarovsky grew up in the small Georgia town of Barnesville, just an hour south of Atlanta. Her love of writing began at the age of eight when she completed her first book about unicorns. Though never published, it was very popular among her peers in school.

As she grew older her passion for writing grew even more. She began writing her first series at age eleven. During her teens she also developed a passion for music. She taught herself how to play the piano, guitar, and bass guitar. She and her brother Scott would spend almost every day writing and performing their own music.

After several failed relationships and nearly giving up on finding her perfect match, she met James on social media. Immediately they fell in love and he took on the role of father to her children. They went on to marry six years later and added more two children to their family.

She began working on *The Watchers* in 2014, inspired by a documentary about fallen angels and the Book of Enoch. During the last several years she has faced many struggles and obstacles that nearly ended her desire to ever write or play music again. Through it all, her sister encouraged her to keep following her dreams and her husband vowed to support her every step of the way.